THE FINDING

BOOK TWO IN
THE CALLING SERIES

L.C. PYE

The Finding

Copyright © 2023 by L.C. Pye

Contact Info: authorl.c.pye@gmail.com

Front Cover Design by: Selkkie Designs

Map Design by: Isabella Whittle

Editor: E&A Editing Services

ISBN: 979-8-9879746-2-9

THE

BOOK TWO IN
THE CALLING SERIES

FINDING

L.C. PYE

LiftedLines Press

SIGN UP FOR MY

AUTHOR NEWSLETTER

Be the first to learn about L.C. Pye's new releases and receive exclusive content.

Dedicated to those who are finding healing from their past. Choose how you see yourself.

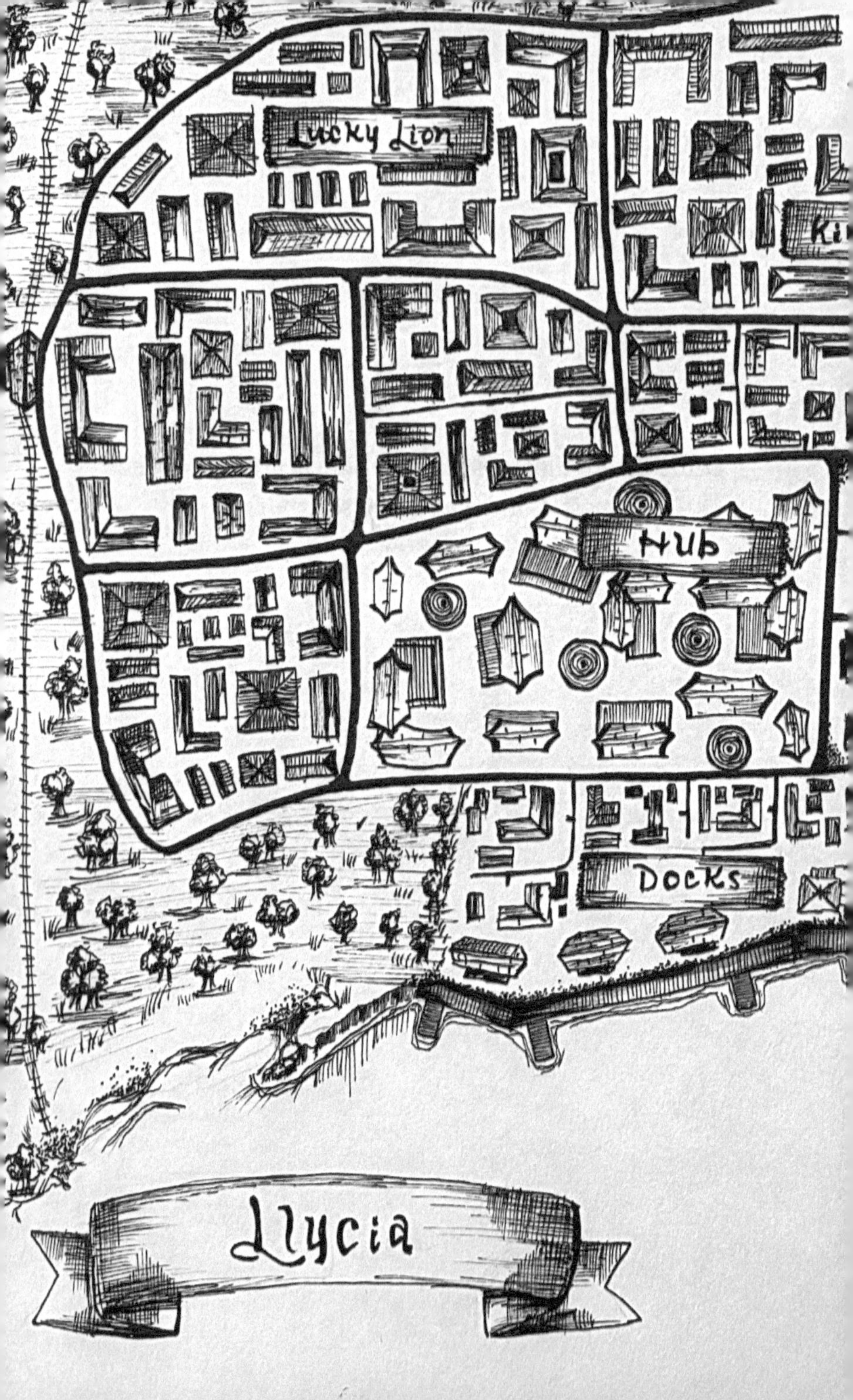

Lucky Lion
Ki
Hub
Docks
Llycia

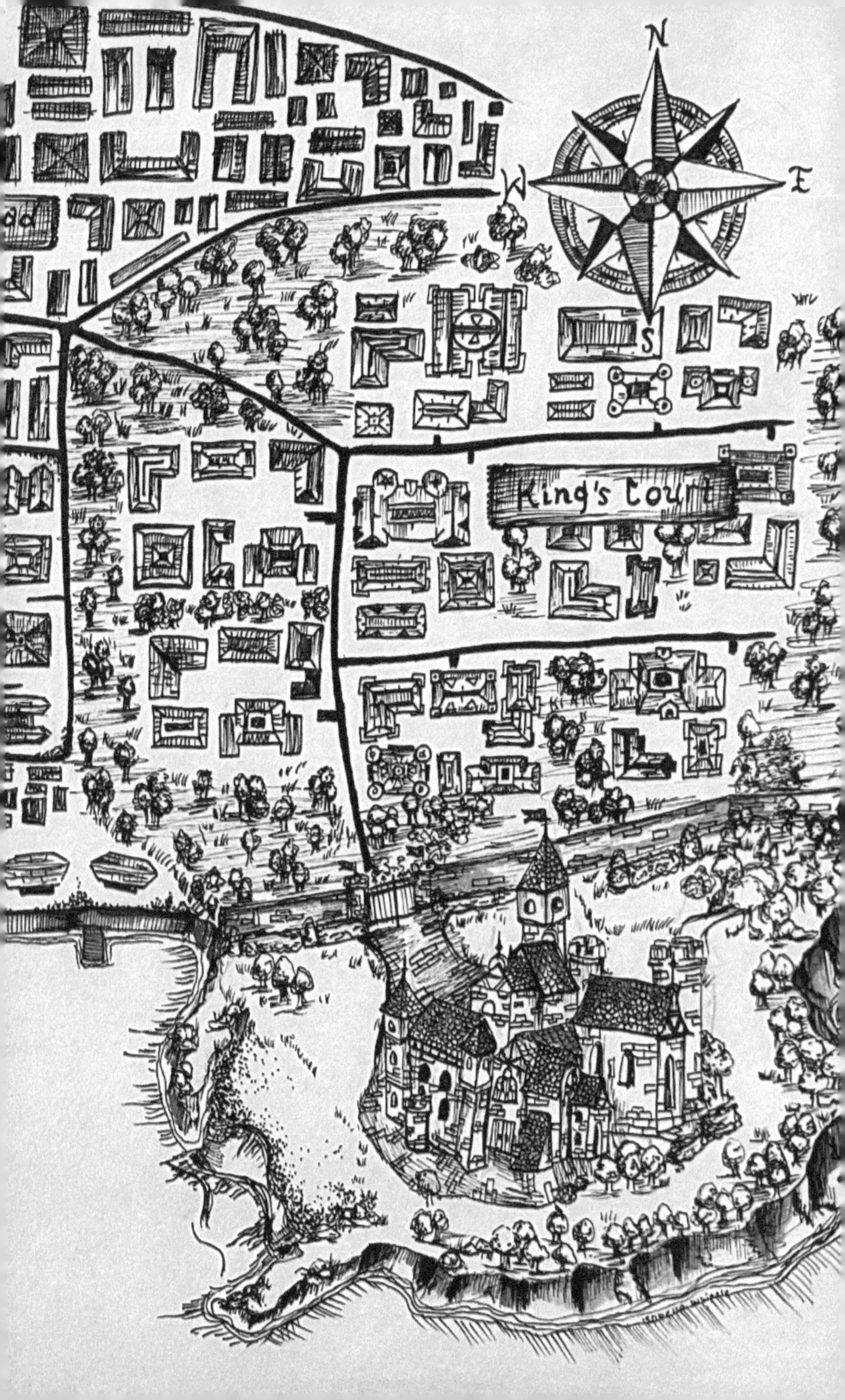

N
E
S
W
King's court

CHAPTER 1

Talia

Loud whooshing filled my ears as if I was trapped in the middle of a storm. And like a cyclone blowing debris around, my mind spiraled on his words, "Now that we have found the lost princess."

A pair of rough hands squeezed my upper arms, yanking me out of my trance by pulling me away as a sinister smile crawled its way across the king's aged face.

"Wait! You've made a mistake."

With flared nostrils and flattened lips, he snapped, "Are you insinuating that I, the king, am wrong?"

The two men holding me came to an abrupt stop, nearly dislocating my shoulder again. My chest heaved as I opened my mouth—

Bang.

The door on the far side of the room flew open. My knees wobbled as fingernails dug into my arms.

King Madden jumped to his feet and roared, "How dare you—"

"Apologies, my king." The unannounced guard bowed deeply and stayed low as he continued, "We have caught a spy within the palace walls."

"Bring them to me at once," King Madden ordered with a flick of his wrist before gesturing for two guards to approach.

He eased back onto his throne and communicated something with the two guards, too low for me to hear. When he finished, his eyes darted up, finding me instantly. They widened slightly before settling to reveal wrinkles in the corners of his eyes. A shiver raced down my spine as his smile broadened, then he fixed the rings on his hands. "This is something I wish for you to see."

My stomach dropped, and I was shoved forward. He watched my every forced step, stroking his graying beard the whole time. I broke from his stare as the far doors creaked open again. The same guard entered leading a slender man, limping, with his arms tied behind his back. The man's shaggy auburn hair covered his face and his eyes stayed on the floor. Behind him, two more guards followed an arm's length away.

My heart rate spiked as I recalled Crazy Old Pete's tales of King Madden's cruelty.

"We found him snooping around the northern side of the palace, my king," the guard in front announced.

"What is his station?" King Madden's eyes hadn't left the man. It reminded me of the time Jules and I watched a black wolf hunt a deer we had been tracking. They shared the same eerie stillness in their eyes.

"He works in the gardens."

"Why then, gardener, would you be inside the palace snooping around where you don't belong?" The man remained silent, staring at his feet. "Look at me!"

His head lifted.

I gasped. He was young. He couldn't have been older than me. It was hard to tell for sure with his bruised and swollen face.

"Are you with the Northern Rebels?" King Madden's voice had calmed a fraction, but the young man remained silent, staring blankly at him. King Madden shot up and marched down the stairs. "You will answer your king!" He raised his hand and slapped the man across the face.

I cringed as blood splattered on the floor.

"You'll never be my king," the man croaked.

King Madden drew his sword and sliced. The young man fell instantly, and angry red line across his throat gushed more blood onto the white stone floor. The silence that followed was oppressive.

A cry broke out. It took me a moment to realize it was my own. I flailed and twisted beneath my guards' grips, trying but failing to break free. All the while, King Madden wiped the man's blood off his sword calmly with a rag. I gave up on my sad attempt to get away and squeezed my eyes shut, unwilling to look at the horror of it one moment longer.

"Leave us," King Madden commanded.

My legs buckled and I dropped painfully to the ground. The sight of red specks on my pants filled my mouth with bile. I attempted to run again, to seize the opportunity, but my arms gave out as I tried to press myself up. When I got my feet under me, his calculating eyes held me where I stood.

"Well, Little Fawn, the question is, are you worth the trouble?" he asked, stalking closer—one heavy boot after the next. "I planned to kill you once I found you. A part of me still thinks that's what I should do..." The scent of spiced liquor hit my face.

I didn't know if he wished for me to answer. It didn't matter. I was frozen like an animal about to be shot.

"Nonetheless." He broke our eye contact. The breath inside my lungs released as he walked around me. "My advisers think you could be of use to me." His steps grew faint. I wasn't sure if I should turn and follow. It seemed my legs decided for me, rooting me to the floor.

"Bring my son!" King Madden yelled, and I turned around. But he continued before the fear surrounding the rumored prince could take hold, "I'm sure you have a swarm of questions in that pretty little head of yours." His gait was slow and predatorial as he made his way back to me.

"This is a big misunderstanding," I croaked. "I'm only a commoner. I'm...I'm no one special. I'm not a lost princess. You've got the wrong person..."

"Never question me." His eyes darkened as he drew closer.

I cowered, taking two steps back.

A sly smile formed on his thin, dry lips. "I see value in you."

I opened and closed my mouth, trying to find the right words to convince him I wasn't who he was searching for.

"You look just like her," he remarked. For a brief moment a shadow flashed over his eyes, but he blinked it away. "You're much taller than she was." He circled me again, close enough to cause the hairs on my arms to rise. "Your golden hair and pale blue eyes are indisputably hers."

"Hers?" I whispered, reaching up to grab my hair, which was hanging in clumps over my shoulders.

"Keep up, Little Fawn." His voice was low with a hint of amusement. "If you want to survive, you're going to have to catch on quicker." He passed by me and returned to his throne.

But what he was suggesting was unfathomable...impossible. None of it could be true.

"I promise, I'm no one." I squeaked out, my fingers moved to my neck only to remember my necklace wasn't there.

"You're wasting my time." He exhaled. "But I'll indulge you, this once." His unrelenting glare told me not to test him. "Do you know your birth parents?"

My mouth went dry.

"Well, no—"

"Has anyone said where you came from?"

"No. But that doesn't mean..."

"Let me guess. You were abandoned somewhere. Left alone. Unwanted. Maybe in a forest close to the border of a village?"

I clenched my fists as my lungs constricted. It didn't prove anything.

"And I can only imagine that throughout your life you've always wondered why no one seemed to look like you." He leaned forward, almost eager. "Why were you the only one with blonde hair, fair skin, and pale blue eyes?"

I shook my head, but I couldn't form a coherent thought.

"I can give you the answers you've been searching for." He reclined and casually crossed his legs. Something deep inside of me, something that I thought was long gone, flickered in my chest. I glanced up.

A smirk appeared on the king's face. "Your grandmother wasn't from here. She was brought here from another kingdom to marry your grandfather, the late king. And you, Little Fawn, carry the physical traits of her people."

"How do I know you're telling the truth?" I said, wrapping my arms around my waist.

"Why would I lie to you?"

"To...to..." I dropped my head as my voice faded out.

"I'm only trying to help you understand." His words were coated with sweetness, but they sounded bitter to my ears.

"What do you want from me?"

He steepled his fingers in front of his mouth. "Now that is the right question."

Before King Madden could answer, the groan of one of the doors filled the room.

"For once your timing suits me." King Madden removed his stare from me and focused on whoever had entered. "Son, come meet your cousin officially, the lost princess."

"What?" I spun to face the newcomer.

It couldn't be. He no longer wore the crimson uniform, instead, he wore head-to-toe black, a personification of what plagued little kids' nightmares. His straight, black hair was a mess. It covered most of his face and touched the nape of his neck.

King Madden waited until he approached the throne, "Little Fawn, meet Prince Kasper, my son and the heir to the throne."

Prince Kasper stayed trained on the throne, unfazed by the dead body lying next to him or the blood mere inches from his boots. His jaw tightened, which enhanced the scar marring half his face. The very scar I had stared at when he stood in the middle of Jules's family home.

I stepped back, wanting to put as much distance between me and the guard who had played a role in Jules's kidnapping—the rumored-to-be-deadly prince. Other than his obsidian hair color, I hardly saw any resemblance to King Madden. I even tried to find similarities between us but couldn't. Seeming to sense my stare, his deadly, gray eyes found mine, and I jerked back. Instantly, I believed every rumor I had ever heard about the crowned prince and his nickname, the King's Wraith. His eyes were full of hate as they bored down on me, causing my palms to sweat.

"You proved to be incapable of staying discreet by allowing commoners to steal from me," King Madden remarked, causing the prince to move his gaze back to the throne. The muscles in the his neck twitched. But before he could respond, the king continued, "Nevertheless, I will put aside my disappointment for this is a joyous occasion." His unnatural smile sent a shiver through me. "I thought it was due time for me to remind the populace of my benevolence and give them something to rejoice in. I will be hosting a ball." With a flourish, he threw an arm into the air. "It will be to celebrate my son's return to court and also to announce the rescue of my great-niece, the lost princess." His eyes bounced from me to Prince Kasper and back to me with a vicious look. "But most importantly, to show how she and the prince will unite our families."

The room began to sway, or I did.

Prince Kasper, meanwhile, coughed.

"This ball will bring unity to the people and all civil unrest will end," King Madden finished with a final flick of his hand as if to seal the deal.

"Father, you can't be serious–"

"You dare question me?" he snarled. And, to my surprise, Prince Kasper dropped his head, looking more like a small child than the notorious King's Wraith. The king held up his hand to silence him further and said, "It will be done."

"I won't." My voice was low, but there was determination in my words.

Prince Kasper spoke over me, "Father, is marriage truly needed?" His annoyance was barely contained in his words. "Announcing her existence alone will appease the people."

"But for how long? How long will it take before they start demanding that *she* is the rightful heir? That *she* should be on the throne." He gripped the arms of his throne. "You will do this."

Prince Kasper took a step forward, but King Madden raised his hand, halting him. "Don't think I don't know about Lliana." His eyebrow rose, challenging Prince Kasper to deny it. The prince's body tightened next to me as his nostrils flared but he said nothing, letting his father's words cut through him. "You're an even bigger fool than I thought if you believed you could keep her a secret. If you don't go through with this, her blood will be on your hands."

The edges of my mouth pulled down as I looked back and forth, trying to understand how a father could threaten his son so. I would've assumed King Madden would treat his heir better.

"I have decided. It will happen," he declared with the full authority of a king. "Now take her out of here. Mistress Pennier is waiting for her."

Prince Kasper gave a nod of submission and retreated. His hand wrapped around my arm as he went, pulling me hard, nearly causing me to stumble. The moment the doors closed behind us, I twisted my arm out of his grip, and he shoved me forward. I expected to meet the ground, but instead, I fell into someone.

Peering up, I saw a girl's shocked face looking back at me, and she wasn't alone. Two other women stood next to her.

"She's your responsibility now," Prince Kasper commanded as he turned his back to me.

"Wait!" I called out, but his steps didn't falter. He was gone, leaving me with thousands of questions coating my tongue.

CHAPTER 2

Raph

THE FAMILIAR RIPE, HEAVY smell, the stone beneath my feet, and the crowds made up of every calling should've made me feel at home, but instead it had my head pounding. It had been seven years since I left these mud-caked streets. I'd sworn I'd never come back. But there I was, because Alon had requested it. I would've said no if anyone else had asked, but I owed him my life. He'd never have asked me to come back unless it was his last option.

I kept to the growing shadows of the towering brick buildings from the impending dusk. No one paid attention to me. Still, I found myself scanning every face that passed, wondering if I recognized any of them.

"Hurry up, the tables are probably full by now." A young man hurried past me, then stopped and turned, impatiently waiting for the man behind him to push through the crowd. The two of them had the eagerness of first timers in Llycia.

They were not alone, Landore's capital's streets were boisterous and overcrowded with people from different villages trying to find a better deal or forget their troubles. And, as the trading hub of Landore, everyone wanted to take part in what it had to offer. Only those approved by the king were allowed to live in Llycia, but many came to visit. What they failed to see, behind the shine of promised fun and riches, was the fetid truth.

It was a show.

Part of me pitied those young men and what awaited them, but there was nothing I could do. Besides, I was on assignment. I leaned against the brick wall, positioning myself across from the most well-known tavern in Llycia. I waited. Countless faces walked by me as time passed. Hope grew in my chest that my old contacts didn't still use the same signals. I preferred not to involve them in our business, but we needed their help. We'd been in Llycia for five days with nothing to show for it.

"You owe me six coppers." A large man yelled, standing near the tavern's doors.

"I won that hand fairly." Another replied.

"You cheated!" The large man swung at the other.

A fight broke out between them. No one attempted to break them up, for it was nothing new. The greed in Llycia choked the vices out of everyone who stepped foot on its streets. The city dangled the false hope of a better life in front of people, but all it ever gave them were empty pockets and regret. I, too, was once naive to its ways. Discovering the truth had been as blinding as being shoved into the light of day after existing in the dark for too long.

I crossed my arms. By the time we get home Alon better share the real reason for not joining us. He said it was too dangerous for Nadav and Hafsa to be in Llycia. They couldn't risk it, being from Nefali. And he needed to help them with something important, so that's why he instructed Adira, Gil, Eitan, and me to do more digging ourselves after returning the kidnapped young women. That was nine days ago, and he never clarified what we were supposed to be looking for. It wasn't uncommon for Alon to share only what he deemed to be necessary. This felt different. My crossed arms tightened at that thought. He had been on edge since the rumors hit that young women were being kidnapped. In the four months since, it only got worse. I'd never seen an ounce of fear in him until Talia Caffrey came into our lives.

The smell of alcohol and body odor pushed its way out of The King's Mead and onto the streets, engulfing me. The shadows grew around me, and I was ready to give up, half relieved that they hadn't shown. I pushed off the wall right as a reflection of light caught my attention.

I waited for it to flicker again to confirm it was coming from a nearby alley, before slithering my way through the people stumbling out of the tavern. I heard nothing because of the muted shouts coming from inside the tavern, but I knew they were there. I wasn't surprised at their reluctance to reveal themselves. They wouldn't until they registered what type of threat I was.

I reached the halfway point of the alley and let out two short whistles followed by a longer one. Silence. Taking a few more steps, I whispered, "Tomorrow will come." I waited unmoving.

Three figures emerged from the shadows to my right. My shoulders raised as three children, no older than I was when I left, approached me hesitantly. The boy in the middle came the closest with his fists clenched, ready for a fight. The other two, a small boy who looked no older than eight and a slender girl who appeared to be the same age as the boy in front of me, hovered near the shadows. I scanned their faces in the limited light.

"Wha' you af'er, grown?" their leader spat. He was tall and gangly like most street orphans who got by on what they could steal. His unwashed curls hung limply over his eyes, and there was a scar above the right side of his upper lip.

"Tommy?" I took a step forward. He reacted by dropping into a familiar fighting stance. "You probably don't remember me," I began again, trying to search his face for that eight-year-old kid who got his lip busted by a Merchant when caught stealing food. "You were so young…"

He simultaneously lowered his hands and his eyes widened as he said, "Raphy?"

I gave him a half smile and a small nod, hiding my cringe at hearing that nickname again. "You've changed. Last time I saw you, you weren't tall enough to look over a stall's ledge. You still giving old Mr. Ferralds a run for his money?" The onslaught of old memories couldn't be held back. Cold nights, empty stomachs, and her screams. I squeezed my eyes to seal that door closed again.

"I can' believe it! Wha' you doin' back? Though' you'd be stale bread." He excitedly waved the other two over. "This is Scat and Lemmy." He gestured to the small boy and said, "Scat spotted you leavin' that message. Though' a grown figured us out." His shoulders relaxed. "Guys, this is *the* Raphy."

Scat's and Lemmy's eyes doubled in size. I'm not sure what stories they had heard about me, but there was awe, and also fear, behind their eyes.

"Uh, yeah. So..." I rubbed the back of my neck. "Tommy, I need your help getting some intel. Intel that a Shade would know." Looking over my shoulder, I lowered my voice. "Do you still have ties to the palace?"

"Things haven' changed that much," he said with mock offense. "Course we got connections. Wha' ya lookin' for?"

"The king is up to something." I gave another glance over my shoulder and shook my head, surprised at how easy it was for me to fall back into old habits, making sure it's still safe and that no poachers were lurking, searching for their next grab.

"Our currency migh' be knowin' stuff, but I'd be a psychic to know wha' that madman is up to." The other two laughed under their breaths as Tommy gave me a mischievous smile, the same one he used to give me when I would get on him for stirring up more trouble than was needed. I dipped my head toward him. "But you ain' wrong," he confessed shoving his hands in his pockets. "Somethin' is goin' down. Our contact ain' confirm anythin' yet, but he's sayin' Madden might be lookin' for a new missus or one for the prince." Before I could comment he continued, "Ladies been seen goin' into the throne room recently."

I rubbed my hand through my hair and sighed. I wouldn't be leaving Llycia anytime soon.

"Wha's goin' on? Wha' you needin' from the king?" He took a step closer, worry traced the edges of his eyes. I shook my head, but Tommy cut in before I could give him an answer. "You know this is wha' we do."

I paced the small alley, trying to find another option—but failing. We needed more intel before we did anything too rash like break into the palace.

"Fine," I gave in with an exhale. "But all I want from you is intel, nothing more."

"I'll reach out when I have somethin'," he answered with a growing smirk.

They turned and melted into the shadows. Tommy's voice called out, "Good to see you, Raphy. Hope you found wha' you was lookin' for."

I pulled back. "What do you mean?"

I was met with silence.

I strolled from the shadows back into the dim light coming from the King's Mead. I mulled over Tommy's words while I walked back to the tavern we were staying at on a quieter side of Llycia. He might have confirmed our suspicions, but I still had nothing new to report to the others. I needed to figure out what I'd say to satisfy them because we'd have to wait to do anything until we got a real lead.

All too quickly, the Lucky Lion came into view. I couldn't put off giving them some sort of report on my meeting.

"Finally! We've been waiting in here for ages," Gil drawled before I had the door fully opened. Adira and Eitan were also stationed in my small room. "Did your contact show?" Gil asked, lounging on my four-poster bed at the far end of the room and throwing daggers at the wooden wardrobe.

Releasing a breath, I shut the door behind me. "Do you have to destroy my room?"

"Maybe you shouldn't have taken so long," he answered with a smirk.

I reclined in a chair near the fireplace since the only other piece of furniture in the room was a small desk near the window. Feeling Gil's eyes bore into me, I couldn't help but take a small amount of satisfaction in his misery. I propped my feet in front of me and supported my head in my hands.

"It's going to get worse if you don't start talking about this mystery contact from your past. The same past that you never talk about..." Gil waved a dagger at me.

Unable to stop the side of my lip from lifting I sat up and recounted the information I had gathered.

"Is your source reliable?" Adira asked. "It's been seven years." Despite standing directly in the shadows, I still caught the telltale pull of her lips, which told me she didn't trust my source. Not that I blamed her. It wasn't that I didn't trust her and the others to not share who my contact was, but some habits were hard to break.

"Yes. They run these streets, and their loyalty, once earned, can never be lost." A bitter taste sat on my tongue, knowing that I didn't deserve their loyalty anymore. "They're the best at what they do."

Her body tensed. "How much longer will we have to stay in this tavern together?" Adira's eyes flicked to her brother who was attempting to balance the hilt of a dagger on his palm.

"I don't know how much longer I can stay cooped up with all of you," Gil added in, not moving his gaze from the dagger.

"It's more important we stay hidden," I answered. "We can't afford to attract unwanted attention by snooping around."

"He's right. The last thing we'd want is for the kidnappers to prematurely recognize us," Eitan chimed in from his place near the door with his arms crossed over his chest.

"Oh, come on. Let's stop beating around the bush," Gil grumbled. "Only the King's Guard would be able to get their hands on those types of weapons and be trained like they were. Plus, that one guard had to be the King's Wraith." His eyes lit up. "And with what your contact said, I'd bet all my coin that the king was behind those kidnappings." He laid back on my bed with his arms behind his head and looked up at the ceiling, placing one leg over the other.

I approached the bed and swatted at his crossed feet, and he jolted upward. I raised my brow when he looked at me, confused by what just happened. Gil had never understood the concept of boundaries.

I paced.

"Do you think he still has some of them locked up in the palace somewhere?" Gil asked with an arched brow. He hadn't left my bed, but at least he had the decency to sit on the edge, his dirty shoes propped up on the frame.

"Unlikely. Especially with the intel we received from Gale," Eitan offered.

Gale was our spy in the King's Guard. He had informed us about the kidnappings and the cruelties of the king. Mainly how the king had no problem offing those who were of no use to him.

"Unless he still plans to use them for something." I stopped pacing and leaned my weight against the chair.

"What could he want with all those young women?" Adira asked, more to herself than the room as she fiddled with one of her throwing knives.

"So, are those we saved truly safe?" Eitan shifted his weight uncomfortably.

I tightened my grip on the chair. My knuckles turned white. "We'll figure it out." I stared into the flames. "We need to wait a little longer. My contacts will be first to figure out what's going on behind the palace doors."

Gil cleared his throat. "Since we have some time to kill, can we talk about why you've been grumpier than usual since leaving Gasmere?" He stared me down with one of his don't-even-deny-it looks.

"Might help if you talk about it," Eitan said.

I turned back to the fire, ignoring their stares, especially Adira's. She read me the best. But I wasn't going to let them know how worried I was for Talia's safety, or that I'd been watching the city gates every morning since we got to Llycia, making sure she hadn't been captured by the King's Guard. I internally groaned. If she was caught with her empty crest, she would've been sent directly to the king for punishment. A shiver traveled down my spine at that thought.

"We don't have time for this," I snapped.

"Whoa." Gil threw his hands up. "Touchy subject."

"Adira," schooling my face, I turned to her, "I want you to watch the palace. Take note of everyone who goes in or out." A part of me was surprised at how readily she nodded. Maybe they weren't as bothered as I was by me making commands.

"Well, you three have fun." She pushed off the mantle and strolled out of the room without another word. I hoped doing what she seemed to love would help her get out of the funk she had been in for the past week.

I turned to Eitan and Gil. "You two go stock up on supplies for our trip home. Keep your heads down and don't talk to anyone," I said the last part directly to Gil who had already jumped from my bed, making his way to the door.

"Don't worry, I'll keep Eitan in line," he said, throwing the door open.

"Make sure he keeps his hood up," I said to Eitan, who gave me a reassuring nod as he followed Gil out.

"We *have* to stop by that shop that smelled like roasted nuts and fresh bread," Gil's voice echoed down the hall.

Rolling my head to the side, I released my breath, ready to be done with it all.

CHAPTER 3

Talia

"FOLLOW, YOUR HIGHNESS," a shrill voice commanded.

My head snapped up at the title. The three ladies were walking away from me. I slowly took a few steps back until I ran into two guards, which told me I had no choice but to follow.

"Keep up," the older woman barked over her shoulder.

I was falling behind, unable to keep up with their treacherous pace. Flashes of red covered my vision. I clutched onto the fabric of my pants, unable to take in any of my surroundings, as I focused on my breathing with each step I took.

They didn't stop until a set of doors blocked the way. Opening the doors they gestured for me to go in first, so I timidly stepped into an enormous space that looked to be a bedroom.

"Come. There's much to be done." The older woman with the shrill voice approached me, and I lifted my hands as I retreated slightly. She stayed put, noticing the small shake in my hands. "We aren't going to harm you, Your Highness," she said, though her tone was anything but reassuring. "We need to clean you up."

This time when she stepped forward, I didn't retreat. The other two also approached. They were much younger and looked as if they could've been the same age as that young spy. My breath faltered as the image of his lifeless face flashed before me.

They ushered me further into the room with quick movements. All I could take in was a bed and a fireplace before they pulled me into another room. They didn't waste time as they grabbed at my clothes.

"What are you doing?" I asked, pulling my tunic back into place.

"We don't have time for this," the older woman answered as she worked on pulling the hem of my shirt up again.

I batted her hand away.

"Your Highness, we need to bathe you." Her stern eyes moved from me to a huge basin I hadn't noticed in the middle of the room. I peered around her and saw hot water pouring into it from a pipe. A deep V formed between my brows.

She reached for me again.

"I can bathe myself." I swatted at her hands. There was no way I was going to let three strangers bathe me.

She sighed. "Fine, but if you aren't out in five minutes, we will come and finish the job." She turned on her heels after shutting off the water and the other two followed in her footsteps. The door shut, and I was finally alone. My blood pulsed in my ears. My hands shook.

I had no idea how to order my thoughts. It was a big misunderstanding. It had to be. For a moment, I wished to be back in that prison cell.

"You have four minutes," she yelled from the other side of the door.

I peeled off my soiled clothes and slowly stepped into the large basin. My muscles screamed in pleasure. The dirt and grim from not bathing for nine days slowly left my skin. I let my body fully submerge in the water. I stayed under until I saw red on white stone.

I broke through the surface and feverishly scrubbed at my pinkish skin, wanting any trace of what had happened to be cleansed away. But what happened to that young man would never leave me.

I'd seen death before, but never had I seen someone murdered in cold blood in front of me. A shudder ran through me. What kind of man was the king? The water no longer felt warm and inviting.

I grabbed a small bottle on a table near the basin and poured its contents over my head. I worked on smoothing out the numerous tangles in my hair. Fighting with one specific knot, I stopped to look at the ends of my blonde hair, one of the things that always marked me as an outsider in my village. The king had said I had "her" hair color. Shaking my head, I continued my work. It wasn't possible.

When I could finally somewhat run my fingers through my hair, I stepped out and grabbed a soft piece of fabric near the bath to cover myself. I didn't see any clothing in the room other than what I wore before, so, timidly, I opened the door.

The three women pounced and put me in some sort of long dress that tied in the front before they ushered me to a chair. The older one walked into an adjoining room while the other two pulled out materials from the vanity I was seated in front of.

While seated I was able to take in more of their appearances. They wore identical charcoal uniforms with white aprons tied around their waists and their hair pulled up tight. However, that was where their similarities ended.

I rubbed the soft silk fabric between my fingers, not sure what else to do while they worked on me. In the mirror, I caught the shorter one, who was brushing out my hair, stealing glances at my face whenever she could. She was curvy with vibrant red hair and a splash of freckles across her face. There was curiosity and amusement behind her brown doe eyes. Yet, every time she stopped working on my hair to stare at me the other one would elbow her in the ribs.

An air of maturity circled her. She stood tall with a slender frame and extremely sharp features in comparison to the round joyful features of her companion. Her hair was jet black and her complexion was dark and flawless. Grabbing some bottles, she applied oils to my skin.

"I can do this myself," I remarked unconvincingly. Neither of them said anything nor did they pause their work. "All of this isn't necessary."

The shorter one pulled back at my words, yanking a good chunk of my hair. "Of course it is! You're the lost princess—"

"Catherine!" rebuked the taller one.

Pulling her lips tight, the shorter one, Catherine, resumed braiding the section of hair she was working on. Still, she continued to glance at me every few seconds. The other one picked up a different bottle and rubbed its contents on my face.

"Are you two Artists?" My question caused her to freeze mid-application. Catherine released a small giggle, which warranted her a glare. Regardless, Catherine seemed unconcerned by her companion's disapproval.

"No, we're your lady's maids, Your Highness." Catherine gave a small bow.

Ignoring her formality, I furrowed my brow.

"Try not to move your face, Your Highness," the taller one scolded while trying to apply a white paste to my face.

"It's kind of hard when you have strangers putting foreign substances on your face," I mumbled because whatever she had put on was beginning to harden.

Catherine snorted, trying to muffle her laughter with the back of her hand.

"What calling do you two belong to then?" I asked, limiting the movement of my lips.

"We don't belong to one of the five, Your Highness," the taller one stated matter-of-factly.

"What?" Cracks covered the mask.

An audible exhale escaped the tall one's lips. Her slender fingers made quick work of pulling the now-hardened pieces off.

"Are you not eighteen years yet?"

"Yes, we are, Your Highness."

"How is that possible?"

"We serve the king, Your Highness. And now you as well. That is our calling."

Her words grew my confusion. I had never thought it possible for people in Landore to not belong to one of the five unless they were a part of the King's Guard.

"What is a lady's maid?" I asked the taller one who had finished peeling off the white paste.

"We are here to—"

"Malenee, what did I tell you?" rebuked the older lady as she reentered the room and walked toward the three of us with an armful of dresses. "Come over here, Your Highness, so I can see how much work must be done to make these dresses fit you." Her words were tight, matching her face.

Catherine and Malenee had finished whatever they were doing with my hair and face. It was styled in a low bun with braids forming a crown around my head. It was impressive. And my face had a soft glow.

Even though the sun had descended, they had me try on dress after dress for what felt like hours, and with each dress, they would make the same comment: they all needed to be let down.

"Catherine, go take these dresses to the workroom and get started."

"Yes, Mistress Pennier," Catherine answered, then walked over to the large pile of dresses. She became buried and struggled to make her way to the door.

"Malenee, will you please..." Mistress Pennier gave a look over her shoulder at Catherine who was trying to pick up a dress she had dropped. Malenee assisted Catherine, and they both left the room, which left me alone with the surly Mistress Pennier.

She walked in circles around me, inspecting me. "Obviously, the king is aware of your upbringing, but at the ball, he will expect nothing less than a true princess." She pulled at a piece of thread on the seam of my sleeve. "This gives us six days to teach you how to appear and act like a proper princess." She finally stopped her dizzying circles and stared me in the eye. "Starting with your understanding of your rank as princess."

"My rank?"

"Yes. You're the Princess of Landore. This means you will not lower yourself by associating with those that are beneath you. You have two maids whose jobs are to serve you meals, help you get dressed, and do whatever other tasks you may ask of them. They, however, are not your confidants."

"Confidants?" I asked, tilting my head.

"You're not to speak to them unless you're giving them commands."

I would have laughed at the absurdity of what she was saying, but thanks to the deep scowl she was giving me, my mouth stayed shut. "Tomorrow you will meet Lady Celeste, she will be one of your ladies-in-waiting. After the ball, you will meet the rest of them. But for now, she will help acclimate you to court life and teach you the proper etiquette for a royal."

"But I'm a—"

"Who you were doesn't exist anymore. You *are* the lost princess of Landore. The sooner you grasp that the easier it will be for everyone involved, *Your Highness*."

A part of me wanted to speak back and say that I didn't ask for any of it, but my words would do nothing. I was under the king's control.

"Do you understand?" She waited for my acknowledgment. I understood her hidden meaning too. If I didn't learn how to become a princess in the next six days, the king's wrath would be on me.

I gave her a small nod, knowing what I needed to do. I needed to find a way to escape.

CHAPTER 4

Raph

AN ELBOW JABBED ME in the ribs as another man to my left almost took me out, swinging a large bag of grain onto his shoulder.

"The finest blades you have ever seen." A Merchant held out a broadsword for me to inspect. "They will cut through anything." The Merchant stepped in front of me, halting my steps. It didn't take but a glance to know it was poorly made with too much weight at the hilt. I'd expected nothing more. Shaking my head, I veered around him, pushing deeper into Llycia's trading hub.

Sweat dripped from my forehead because of the afternoon sun beating against my back and the lack of airflow in the throngs of people. The Hub was the perfect place for a meetup, but all I wanted was the calm of the forest. I made my way over to a stall, feigning interest in the useless wooden trinkets by picking one up. Most of the stalls were like that one, filled with items for villagers to waste their coins on.

Each wooden stall was identical, consisting of four posts that held up a canopy to shade the Merchant. There weren't enough stalls for everyone, so many of the Merchants from other villages spread their goods on rugs.

Tommy approached the stall and picked up a small wooden horse next to me, his auburn curls giving him away. In the daylight, he looked older. He couldn't be over fifteen, but he was only a few inches shorter than me and could have passed for eighteen.

"Impressive," I said under my breath. If anyone heard me, they might have thought I was talking about the wooden trinkets, but Tommy knew I was referring to his ability to get information so quickly.

"Nah, Raphy, you got lucky." He gave me a half smile as he moved behind me. "This news is spreadin' like wildfire," he whispered, passing to the other side of the stall.

I gave the Merchant, who was convincing an older lady to buy a pair of wooden doves, a curt nod, and turned away. After a few moments Tommy followed behind me.

"My boy don' know much 'cept everyone is in a tizzy over somethin'. Or should I say...someone." Over my shoulder, I caught him wiggling his eyebrows at me. "Keepin' a tight lid on it, but my boy overheard that the king is announcin' somethin'. Doin' it at a public ball."

I stopped walking, and Tommy slammed into my back. "Are you positive your contact is correct?" I asked, quickly turning to inspect some tunics hanging from another stall. Madden had never thrown a ball before, at least not a public one. He was notorious for throwing elaborate parties, but they were for nobility and the higher class.

"Yah, but it isn' really open to everyone. Only invitin' the heads of each village." Tommy picked up a sand-colored tunic and then placed it back, simultaneously shoving a smaller one under his shirt. It was so smooth that I barely noticed it. It was a move I taught him many years ago. He winked as he turned to leave. I followed, but not before I threw a few coins on the pile he took from.

"This isn't normal, right?" I asked once I was close enough for him to hear me.

"Nah. Think he got somethin' big he needs spreadin' fast."

I ran a hand down my face, already sensing that I'd have to figure out how to crash that ball with the others.

Following behind Tommy, I recognized his head swerving back and forth as a telltale sign that he was about to slip away. I grabbed his forearm before he could and slid a bag of coins into his hand. "Take care of them and know that there will always be a place for you," I whispered.

He shook his head and slipped the bag into his pocket before anyone else could see. "Someone has to stay behind and help the fresh meat."

I watched his curls disappear into the crowd with a knot in my stomach. Shades were family, but the moment Alon offered me a better life, away from here, I took it without saying goodbye. Part of me hoped this would be the last time I saw Tommy. I wasn't sold on involving kids in our mission as the right choice, no matter how resourceful they were. Plus, every time I saw him, I was reminded of *her*.

Someone bumped into my back, bringing me into reality. If I didn't get back to the rendezvous site soon, Gil would come searching for me, not out of concern, but as an excuse to "see the sites."

Walking through the familiar shadows, I pondered over the new information. Alon had made it clear that he wanted to know exactly what Madden was up to because if the rumors were right, everything was about to change, not just for Aydencia though. It would impact all of Landore.

As I opened the doors of the King's Mead, I easily spotted Gil and Eitan sitting at a back table. Our best option was to get at least one of us into that ball. The real problem was how to do it.

"Do you have to eat all the rolls? I know you're huge, but, come on, some of us would like to eat too!" Gil's voice cut through the noise of drunk patrons as he stole a roll from Eitan's plate.

"You know that I eat when I'm anxious," Eitan replied with his mouth full. I grabbed the open seat between them.

"Next time, I'm coming with you," Gil stipulated, ripping a piece of bread between his teeth. He was on edge. We all were.

"Did you notify Adira?" I asked while I rubbed my thumb along the handle of the mug a passing barmaid placed in front of me.

"She should be here any minute," Gil confirmed as the table next to ours broke out in cheers.

It was early in the evening, but the King's Mead was as busy as ever. We picked the place because of that, but all the noise was adding to the pressure in my head.

Grabbing the drink in front of me, I chugged the watered-down ale. Adira needed to show up soon, I wouldn't last much longer.

"Another?" asked a different barmaid.

"No," I said, dismissing her with my hand.

"I'd love another, and maybe you could bring us more rolls," Gil said with a wink. The barmaid giggled, before walking away.

I turned my sharp gaze at Gil. We were taught to keep a clear head. You never knew when trouble might walk through the door.

"What? The drink is for Adira, and I'm hungry," he said.

We turned our heads as the bell on the front door jingled. Adira strolled through. She found us immediately and a small smile pulled at the corner of her mouth. Then I saw who was following behind her.

CHAPTER 5

Jules

SINCE STEPPING FOOT IN Llycia, I felt like a fish out of water. The voices were deafening, and the smell of liquor and body odor hit me. I retreated a few steps. Grabbing the string of my bow around my chest, I advanced.

"Hey, beautiful. You can join our table," a man called out, slurring his words as I weaved through the tables. I didn't look in his direction. Instead, I kept my focus fixated on the hooded beacon of hope in front of me.

Adira was elbowing her way through the crowd like she did it every day of her life. I picked up my pace, following through the openings she had made. She stopped abruptly, causing me to nearly run into a woman carrying a tray of drinks. It wasn't until I collected myself that I saw the reason for the halt.

Three familiar faces sat in front of us. My attention went to Gil first, who looked like a fish, his mouth open and eyes bulging. His head jerked back and forth from Adira to me. Eitan was more subtle, raising one brow in our direction. Yet their expressions weren't the ones that worried me. It was the broody one next to Gil who looked like he was ready to fight someone.

"You can all take a breath and relax," Adira said, breaking the silence. She grabbed the chair next to Gil, leaving me the one next to Eitan.

"Why is she here?" Raph demanded, refusing to look in my direction.

"*She* has a name," I snapped back. "Man, Adira was right. You are a grump." Leaning back in the chair, I gave him an amused smirk.

Gil and Eitan tried (and failed) to suppress their laughter. Raph scowled at Adira harder and rubbed one of his temples.

"No need to get so worked up," she stated with a smirk forming on her lips. "You told me to keep an eye on the palace. That was what I did." She grabbed the half-eaten roll in her brother's hand. Gil's mouth dropped in offense, but before he could complain, she continued, "Not too many people were coming in or out, but there was one person who kept hanging around the palace gates. So, I investigated," she shrugged, "and was just as shocked when I found out who it was." She finished by taking a bite.

Raph turned his attention to me. He raised his eyebrows, clearly expecting me to explain myself.

I crossed my arms. "Your 'tough-guy glare' isn't going to work on me. I'm not telling you anything until you share why you four are here. Adira," I turned my glare onto her, "is being annoyingly tight-lipped."

"No," Raph said. At the same time a young woman set two more drinks down on the table along with a basket of bread rolls.

I picked up the mug in front of me and gave Raph a small noncommittal shrug, trying to hide my desperation.

"Raph, come on, it's Jules." Gil leaned over to Raph and whispered something I couldn't hear over the noise around us. Whatever it was had Raph on edge because he cleared his throat and crossed his arms, before looking back at me.

"Fine," he relented.

I took a drink to help me swallow the lump of anxiety in my throat before raising an eyebrow back at Raph.

Releasing a sigh, he began to share, "We had suspicions that those outlaws who kidnapped you and the other young women weren't average criminals." He was giving the bare minimum.

"I assumed as much," I said. "They were too organized and well trained. Plus, one of them had a sword that was way too fancy for a common criminal. So do you think they were hired by someone?" I set the mug down.

"Alon had theories from the start that the king might be involved," Raph continued. "He ordered us to come to Llycia and figure out what exactly Madden was up to."

"The king ordered—"

Eitan clamped his hand on my shoulder, causing me to jump in my chair. "Sorry," he apologized. "It is for the best that we don't go around making such claims." I dipped my head, placing my shaking hands underneath my legs.

"But why would he do that?" I whispered.

"Your turn," Raph stated.

"But that can't be all," I argued. "You definitely know mo—"

"That is all I am sharing for now." His gaze was unyielding.

"I don't understand what she sees," I mumbled before letting out an exasperated exhale. "Our village Elders learned that we had returned." I leaned forward, and they mimicked my movement. "According to my parents, who are also Elders, they decided to perform Talia's ceremony in secret the following morning, but somehow, the King's Guard found out. They came for her before the ceremony could take place." My voice cracked. Eitan raised his hand as if to comfort me, but placed it back down. "They took her. I could do nothing but watch it happen." Coughing, I briefly closed my eyes. "But I couldn't...I couldn't stay in Gasmere, not knowing...not when she had risked her life for mine."

I played with my hands in my lap while I waited for one of them to say something.

"Have you found out anything?" Eitan asked.

"No." I dropped my head. "I asked a few people on the street when I got here, what happened to people who didn't choose a calling." I could feel the tension of the group rise at my words, but no one said anything. "Most said she could've been placed as a palace servant. So I went to the palace gates and asked every servant that came in or out if they'd heard of a servant named Talia, or even seen someone that looked like her." I narrowed my eyes, still frustrated at the responses. "Most of them just scurried away, blatantly ignoring my questions. A few acknowledged me with a shake of their head, but they wouldn't speak. It was like they were terrified of me or something." Burning with determination, I focused on Raph. "I need to get into that palace."

He sat unmoving while everyone stared at him with tight faces. "We will see what we can find out, but I think it's best if you go—"

"Don't you say it!" I slammed my palms onto the table not caring who overheard me. "I'm not leaving until I've found Tals." My hair clung to the nape of my neck, but my insides felt cold and hollow. However, I didn't let my fear show as I held Raph's stare. I wouldn't give them any choice but to allow me to help. I was getting into that palace.

"You have to follow my orders," he over pronounced each word.

"Done."

I looked over at Adira, expecting her support, but her eyes were locked on Raph. All three of them were looking at him with widened eyes.

Raph ignored them as he continued, "The people you talked to aren't wrong. If she was taken by the King's Guards for missing her calling ceremony, she belongs to the king as his property."

"Will she be in the palace somewhere?" I asked.

Adira's head twitched, drawing Raph's attention. Some form of communication passed between them as they stared each other down. Breaking from Adira, he said, "Most likely."

He told the others about some meeting he had with an old contact. He didn't take the time to fill me in, but I hadn't expected him to. However, the moment he mentioned the possibility of other women being locked away, my heart skipped a beat. His words became distant, and it took all my concentration to focus on my breathing.

"A ball, you say?" Gil's voice rang through the fog, as he shimmied his shoulders and fixed his tunic.

Shaking my head, I held my breath before releasing it.

"We need to split our focus on two areas the night of the ball," Raph continued. "Two of us will take up residence in the ballroom to hear whatever the king's announcement will be. The other three need to scour the palace looking for any young women that might still be held captive."

"And find Tals," I added.

"Yes, if she isn't a servant, then she'll be with the captive women if they are still—"

"What you're saying is we need covers to get into the palace?" Eitan interrupted. "Not to mention, a big enough diversion to get not only ourselves but anyone else who might be held captive out."

Raph lowered his head toward Eitan.

"And a quick getaway if things turn south," Adira added.

"Yes," Raph confirmed.

"We might need some extra help on this one." Gil said, scratching the side of his head.

"We'll go scope out the palace tomorrow night, and I'll set up another meeting," Raph explained.

They seemed to relax a little as they nodded their heads to his plan.

"You can stay with me if you want," Adira offered. "I have an extra bed in my room."

"Thanks," I said, accepting her offer.

"Just have to warn you, she snores," Gil said, leaning over Adira.

Adira shoved him away. "After this mission, I don't want to see you for a month."

"Tough luck, Sis, you know Mother and Father aren't going to let us out of their sight for days." He threw his arm around Adira. "They are a tad bit overprotective," he said to me.

A barmaid stopped by, dropping off bowls of stew. Everyone dug in, Adira and Gil continued their banter, but my mind was back in Gasmere, replaying that moment when the guards took Tals away, and I just stood there in the road, frozen. After failing those other women, I swore I would never let something like that happen again, and not even a day later, Tals was taken. I placed my spoon back down as my hand trembled.

I had to leave Gasmere. I had to fix everything. I had to save Tals.

Chapter 6

Talia

A SHARP INHALE NEARBY jolted me from my sleep. My eyes ached from the light pouring into the room, so I squeezed them shut again and pulled the blanket over my face. It did next to nothing to fix the pounding in my head.

"Your Highness, what are you doing on the floor? Is the bed not suitable?" A familiar shrill voice echoed through the room. Reality sank in real fast after that. I rolled over to sit up, wincing at the pain in my back. I'd opted for the floor knowing I'd sleep better next to the fire, but I was regretting that decision. Mistress Pennier stood ramrod straight with a disapproving stare as Catherine and Malenee looked on in horror from behind her.

She spoke again, "We're here to get you ready for the day. Would you mind getting off the floor, Your Highness?"

Rubbing the base of my neck, I rolled out a kink, but made no effort to get up. "Thank you, but I won't be needing your assistance. I'm perfectly capable of getting ready myself."

Catherine swayed on her heels, but Malenee and Mistress Pennier didn't react.

"It doesn't matter what you're capable of. A princess does *not* get herself ready." She countered my dismissal with a locked jaw and tightened muscles in her neck.

"What if I don't want to be a princess," I mumbled under my breath.

"There's no time to argue about this." She drew closer, giving the impression that she was about to pull me up from the ground herself. "Your maids *will* dress you. I will be back with Lady Celeste to start your training—Your Highness," she tacked that on at the end.

I stood with an exhale, allowing the warm blanket to fall. Wrapping my arms around my waist, I gazed at the dead fire. Catherine laid a thick cloak over my shoulders, and I allowed her and Malenee to usher me to the ivory chair in front of the vanity. My shoulders relaxed when Mistress Pennier finally left.

Malenee pulled out countless items, covering the surface of the vanity. There were different colored rouges and powders, little trays of charcoaled pencils, and vibrant paint palettes. To me, it looked like an Artist was about to create something. She got to work applying things to my face while Catherine's gentle hands took out the braids, she had done for me last night.

I stared at the lilac walls in front of me, following the gold spiral design all the way to the ceiling, which reached higher than the broken windmill inside the Farmer's quarter, about twenty feet. The whole room was ridiculous, easily six times the size of my bedroom in Gasmere. It made me feel uneasy.

I peered through the mirror at Catherine and Malenee. "Do you both believe I'm the lost princess?"

Their hands froze, and they stared at each other silently.

Malenee spoke first. "Your Highness, it's not our job to converse in such a way with you. When Lady Celeste comes, you—"

I threw my hands in the air. "I couldn't care less about what is appropriate or not. It's ridiculous to think that you two will be with me almost every waking moment and I can't talk to you. Can you also please stop with the whole 'Your Highness' thing after *every* sentence."

Catherine dropped her hands from my hair, mouth agape as she stared at me. But the only sign of emotion Malenee gave was her hand clutching the charcoal pencil.

"We're following orders, Your Highness," Malenee said with a bow.

"They're ridiculous and pointless. I have more in common with you two than some Lady," I said softer, looking at my hands.

They continued their work.

"Yes, we do, Your Highness," Catherine answered my question with a whisper so Malenee couldn't hear. A small smile flitted across my lips as I let them finish.

I averted my eyes from my reflection, not even recognizing myself when they were done. They led me to the small room that's sole purpose was to house dresses. They picked out a simple copper-colored dress that billowed out around the waist. The sleeves were just shy of my wrists, and the hem landed right above my ankles. I scratched the fabric as it rubbed my arm, then pulled down on the high-neck collar.

"We're still working on your other dresses, Your Highness. They'll be done today," Catherine offered while Malenee finished buttoning the back of the dress.

Knock. Knock.

Malenee made quick work of approaching the door, however, Mistress Pennier pushed it open herself the moment Malenee turned the handle.

"Great, you're ready," she said, giving me a small bow as she entered. "Princess Talia, allow me to introduce you to Lady Celeste, your lady-in-waiting." She stepped to the side to reveal what, in my mind, I thought a princess should look like.

Lady Celeste floated toward me and the only sound came from the satin fabrics of her royal blue dress brushing together. It had a billowing skirt that cinched her waist, giving her an hourglass figure. Her dark brown hair was pinned up in an elaborate hairstyle, showing off her round delicate face. She stopped before me and bowed with more grace than I had ever seen in my entire life. A petite smile formed on her red lips as she lifted her head to look at me.

I pulled at my sleeves and shifted my weight.

"It's such an honor, Your Highness." Her voice was melodic as it drifted across the room.

"And what is she here for?" I asked, still in somewhat shock.

Mistress Pennier's face hardened. "Your Highness, that is no way to speak—"

"It's okay." Celeste placed her hand on Mistress Pennier's arm. "I'm here to help you adjust to court life, to teach you proper etiquette, and to be a friend."

It took everything in me not to scoff at her obviously rehearsed pitch. She continued to smile at me, causing the hair on my arms to raise.

"Lady Celeste is the daughter of one of the highest-ranking members of the court. She is the perfect candidate for one of your ladies-in-waiting," Mistress

Pennier explained, as if that changed everything. "She has been taught everything a princess would need to know." Celeste's smile faltered, but only briefly before she schooled it back into place.

"I will leave you in her capable hands." Giving me a stern gaze, Mistress Pennier bowed, and exited the room.

Silence followed.

Shifting my weight from the balls of my feet to my heels, I fiddled with my thumbs. I peered over my shoulder to Catherine and Malenee who were standing at the edge of the room staring blankly ahead.

"So..." I said.

"Have you eaten yet, Your Highness?" Her voice was still musical, but there was a new sharper tone to it.

"No."

"We will start there then." Her smile dropped instantly, and she turned to Catherine and Malenee. "Bring Her Highness and me some breakfast."

They gave a small nod, then turned to bow to me before shuffling out of the room.

"They must still be working on your wardrobe." She stood in front of me with her hands clasped. The look in her eyes was all too familiar. It was the same look I received from the girls in Gasmere—distaste. Heat traveled up my neck, I hadn't asked for her help and especially not her scrutiny. "While we wait, we can work on your posture."

It wasn't soon enough when a faint knock rapped against the door. My whole body relaxed the moment I saw Malenee and Catherine enter pushing a cart. They brought it over to where Celeste and I were already seated at a small table.

"We'll move on to dining etiquette, but you must maintain your posture," Celeste chided as if pretending I had a knife in my back for the past half hour hadn't been torture enough.

Catherine and Malenee unloaded the cart and placed cutlery and dishes on the table. Finally, they placed a large platter filled with all sorts of pastries, fruits, and other items I had never seen before. When they finished, they both took a step back and stood silently with their hands clasped behind them.

"Thank you. It looks delicious," I said with a smile even though my stomach felt like it had a large rock in it.

"Oh, Your Highness." Celeste stared at me from across the table. "Never thank the help."

"Why not?" I didn't try to hide the annoyance in my voice.

"It's their job to serve you. You don't need to thank them for it."

Defiantly I turned to where Catherine and Malenee stood and said, "Thank you," again.

Celeste's mouth opened before she slammed it shut. I had to bite the inside of my cheek to stop the smile from forming.

"You may begin, Your Highness." Nothing was musical about her voice anymore. My throat went dry as I stared at my filled plate and the endless cutlery. There was a bemused smirk on her lips. "I can't eat unless you take the first bite."

Returning her fake smile with one of my own, I grabbed the closest pastry with my hands and took a large bite. I forced myself to swallow as it turned to ash in my mouth. The stunned look on her face was worth it.

"It's not...not proper for a princess to eat that way."

"Well, it's the only way I know how to eat. I didn't want you wasting away as I tried to figure it out." Giving a tilt of my head, I took another bite.

Her lips pressed together into a flat line. After a slow breath, she forced them to lift ever so slightly. "Let's start over, shall we?"

"After you."

She spent the next hour teaching me the proper etiquette for eating. It felt like a different language. There were so many rules like never eat before the king takes his first bite, never speak above a whisper to the person next to you, and *never* take big bites. None of that had anything to do with the cutlery placed beside the plate. I couldn't believe it when she recounted the specific use for each one. It would take forever to remember them all.

"Let's move on. We will try again at lunch," Celeste said between her teeth, after I failed at reciting the correct usage of the three different spoons again.

"Start again," Celeste ordered from behind my shoulder. I sat at a desk she'd had Malenee and Catherine bring into the room to help with my training.

"The Kingdom of Landore had always known peace and abun...abund—"

"Abundance," Celeste corrected for the hundredth time. She was having me read from one of the few books still around, which contained our kingdom's history.

King Madden had banned all books when he ascended the throne, claiming they had been doctored by the late king, so I never learned to read well. My parents taught me the best they could, but not having any books to practice with prohibited me from progressing too much. Many villagers my age or younger didn't know how to read at all. It seemed that with each year the ability to read and write diminished.

When Celeste first placed the book in front of me, I was speechless. I never thought I would get the chance to not only hold a book but read from it. Celeste's first lesson had been on how King Madden's first act as king was to close the borders to our neighboring kingdoms. It was believed that one or all of them had murdered the royal family while they were visiting for a renewal of a peace treaty, which was something I already knew. His second order, before the uprisings, was to declare that all books were to be burned. If anyone was found with one, they would be deemed a traitor. The punishment for treason was death.

"Abundance. Landore used its im...imm...ense resources, lumber and animal furs, to trade with the three other kingdoms, accepting priceless gems, metals, rice, and coffee in exchange. What's coffee?" I asked as a yawn escaped my lips. A giggle escaped Catherine, but she muffled it after Celeste's heated stare. I had been reading for hours, and my eyes were watering.

"It's a dark, bitter drink that gives one a lively feeling. It's a favorite of the king," Celeste answered, pleased with herself. She was seated in front of me and was working on weaving thread in and out of a piece of fabric.

"If we no longer trade with the other kingdoms, how does he get coffee? And how do you know so much about Landore's history?"

"Everyone at court has been taught this since they could walk," Celeste answered. "And King Madden always finds a way to get what he wants." She peered up at me and pushed the needle into the fabric harder than necessary.

"No one in the villages is taught any of this," I said, flipping through the numerous pages. "We're taught a muddled-down summary of how everything is much better and safer for Landore with King Madden on the throne."

"That is all peasants need to know," she scoffed, then resumed her work.

My hands shook. "Well, I'm one of those 'peasants'."

She calmly removed the fabric from her lap and placed it in a basket before turning her fiery stare to me. "Not anymore. You're Princess Talia, fiancée to the crown prince and our future queen. And nothing will change that." Her face reddened as she flexed her fingers before taking a slow breath. "I think we're done for the day, Your Highness. I will be back in the morning to continue your training." Without another word, she dismissed herself.

I sat in my chair, perplexed by her outburst. The last thing I wanted was to be princess. I would rather die than marry Prince Kasper.

"Your Highness, are you ready to turn in for the night?" Malenee's voice startled me. I had forgotten they were still in the room. They hadn't said anything all day, besides to agree with whatever Celeste commanded them to do.

"Yes, but I would like to do it myself. I need some time...alone."

"But Your Highness—"

"We will give you some peace and quiet," Catherine spoke over Malenee, communicating something to her with her eyes.

"Of course," Malenee relented. "Just tell the guard outside your door if you need anything, and he will notify us."

I pushed against the back of the chair still frustrated about having discovered the guard last night. They closed the giant golden curtains over the enormous windows and took their leave.

I ran to the bed grabbing a pillow and screamed into it as loudly as I could. It was hopeless, but I couldn't do nothing. I needed to find a way to escape. The idea alone pushed me into action, and I frantically searched the room. There had to be another way out. Last night I was too distraught to think straight, but a new determination was coursing through my veins. Pulling back the heavy curtains, I fiddled with the latch on the window. I realized they were actually two doors that opened up to a small balcony.

A strong gust of wind pushed me back, and I had to use all my strength to keep the doors from slamming against the wall. When the gust eased, I slipped out, closing the door behind me. The chill of the night air seeped into my bones, but I breathed in a huge lung full anyway. It felt like the first real breath I had taken in days.

The taste of the salty air solidified my resolve for freedom. The palace was located on a cliff backing up to the ocean, and I could hear the waves crashing against the rocks in the distance. Peering over the side, my stomach flipped. I was on the third story. There was no way I could jump and survive the landing. The sides of the castle were smooth, and there were no crevices for me to scale down. What I needed was rope.

And it hit me. There was an endless supply of rope in the room.

After the tenth dress, I gave up counting and resorted to tying every dress from the small room together. I silently thanked whoever had altered them for their speed and hoped it would be long enough. What I wouldn't have done for Raph's dagger to cut the dresses to make them longer.

Carefully opening up the doors, I pushed the pile of dresses turned rope onto the balcony. I tied one of them to a short column on the balcony's railing and threw the rest of them off the side. Without overthinking, I climbed over the stone railing and clung onto the first dress with all my might. It wouldn't be hard for someone to spot me, so I shimmied down quickly. I didn't look at the ground until I was holding onto the last dress. Thankfully, it was a few feet off the ground, so I let go and fell to my knees as my legs absorbed the impact. I pushed off the ground and flattened myself against the palace wall, trying to stay within its shadow. I scanned the grounds, not knowing which direction would be best for me to take. To my right was the ocean and to my left were gardens.

Voices came from my right, making the choice for me. Sprinting, I flung myself behind the first hedge I saw, scraping my arms in the process. I stayed low and close to the hedge, moving farther away from the voices. No doubt someone would have spotted my rope made out of dresses. The whole place would be swarming with guards.

I followed the curve of the hedge, keeping my sights on the palace until I bumped into a hard surface. A grunt escaped my lips when I landed on my backside.

"Isn't this interesting."

CHAPTER 7

Talia

PRINCE KASPER'S DEEP VOICE rang through my ears, and my heart jumped into my throat. His face was covered by the shadows of the night, but his clenched fists told me everything. He reached for me, and I pushed myself backward on the wet grass. He kept his arm extended, offering me assistance, but I declined.

"What are you doing out here?" he asked while I righted myself.

Fear and defeat muted me. His face was no longer hidden. I took in his disheveled appearance, trying not to imagine what errand he must've been on as the King's Wraith.

"I-I was getting...fresh air." His silent stare made my hands tremble.

"And you decided that climbing off your balcony, using dresses, was the best way to do that?"

I grimaced as I peered over my shoulder to see my rope of dresses blowing in the distance. Along with red beacons running around the palace grounds as the King's Guard searched for me.

"Your Highness," a guard yelled, approaching from behind the prince. "Th-the princess has es-scaped," he stammered out in between breaths.

"I noticed," Prince Kasper said, stepping to the side.

"Oh." The guard's chest heaved. Shaking his head, he continued, "The king desires an audience with her."

Prince Kasper's posture changed ever so slightly at the mention of his father.

"I'll bring her. Leave us."

Desperation took over. "Please, let me go," I begged. "You don't have to do this. Let me go home." Tears streamed down my face.

For a brief moment, the same pain I felt could be seen in his eyes. But he washed it away. "You shouldn't have tried to escape." Grabbing my forearm, he dragged me out of the hedges.

"Why do you do what he says? You don't have to be like him." I stumbled as his grip tightened. He didn't reply. He kept his dark gaze on the palace.

My heart thrummed in my chest as we entered. I frantically scoured my surroundings, trying to find some way out. A few maids passed us, but they dropped their heads and scurried away. With no other options, I threw my weight around trying to wriggle out of his grip. It was futile. He brought me to a stop outside two familiar doors. I swallowed the dry lump in my throat.

"Don't fight back. It will make it worse," he muttered, then pushed the doors open.

The throne room was tall, bare, and windowless. It reminded me of a prison. There were no decorations or paintings, and the walls were neutral. There was nothing to look at besides the king and his ghastly throne. I stuttered to a stop, and my heart beat loudly in my ears, but Prince Kasper kept me moving. The throne looked like a beacon of death, heralding my own. I tried not to focus on the spot where the young man had been dead in his own blood, but that image left me when I caught King Madden's stare.

He was reclined against the deep crimson cushions, and his chin rested on one of his fists as he analyzed me with every step I took. He resembled a painting, unmoving and without a single hair out of place. He still wore the same black velvet coat that came to his knees. It was met by his knee-high leather boots that were also black. The only color on him was the gold clasps securing his coat. When my gaze went back to his face, his beady black eyes narrowed.

"You're tenacious. I'll give you that," he said, once we reached the dais. "But unfortunately, that is not a quality I can afford for you to have." Shaking his head, he stood and leisurely made his way down the steps. "Bring her in," he demanded. Prince Kasper released my arm, and stepped away from me. "Remember, Little Fawn, this is happening because of the choice you made." His voice reflected disappointment, but his eyes danced with excitement.

Sweat coated the nape of my neck. I tried to prepare myself for whatever might happen next, but as the doors opened to reveal a small sobbing Catherine, my resolve shattered. Flashes of the young man's lifeless face mixed with Catherine's had me shaking. A guard brought her before the king. Her red, swollen eyes found me and everything inside me cried out.

"Son, if you will do the honors." King Madden gestured to Catherine.

My head snapped to Prince Kasper who was completely still. His eyes flicked to Catherine and then back to his father before his hand went to the belt on his hip. He unclasped a whip that was coiled there.

"No!" I shouted as he took a step toward her. I ran in front of him, pressing my hands against his chest to stop him. "You can't do this." I turned to face King Madden. "Please, don't do this."

"I'm not. This is your doing." His demeanor darkened as his eyes pierced through me.

"No! I never... I didn't know." A sob broke free. My hands trembled as they still pressed on Prince Kasper's chest. "Take me," I whispered. "Take me instead." My voice hardened with determination as I faced the king with clenched fists.

A genuine smile formed on his lips. "I appreciate your willingness, but I learned long ago that lessons are better learned this way." His eyes darted to his son briefly before returning to me. "Proceed."

"No!" I threw myself in front of Catherine.

"Guard, restrain her," King Madden ordered.

I threw my head back, trying to break out of his clutches, as I was lifted off the ground. His arms squeezed the breath from my lungs.

It didn't stop me from shouting as Prince Kasper drew back his arm and released the whip. Catherine's scream rang out, and blood seeped through her uniform.

My voice became hoarse as I joined Catherine, screaming with each slash. After the last one, I was dropped to the ground, where I stayed. Ten lashes had ripped open her uniform, revealing a marred back. She laid curled on the floor, and her cries were the only sound in the room.

"Remove her," King Madden commanded to the guard who had restrained me.

Unable to move, I watched as she was dragged out of the room. When the doors closed, I turned to Prince Kasper, hoping to find remorse of some kind. He stood with his whip out, staring at the blood splattered against the white stone, but his face was hard and un-repentant, showing me who he truly was—the King's Wraith.

"How unfortunate." King Madden tsked while fixing his rings. "All of that could have been avoided."

A deep and all-consuming fire roared inside me. "How could you?" I pushed up from the ground and stomped toward him.

"It's time you learn, Little Fawn, that you belong to me. I own you. Look at that empty mark on your arm." His nostrils flared. "I can make you do whatever I want. And if this isn't enough..." He gestured to the blood coating the floor. "Don't think for a moment that I wouldn't send guards to Gasmere to burn it to the ground."

My lip trembled as hot tears streamed down my cheeks.

He leaned closer. "No one is out of my reach."

King Madden stalked back to his throne as I sobbed.

"Your refusal to accept what's required of a princess is over. From here on out, I want reports on how you are excelling in your duties." He casually crossed his legs and lifted a chalice to his mouth. His eyes found me over the lip of the cup, demanding my obedience. Unable to stop sobbing, I gave him a small nod.

"Wonderful, now we can put this all behind us. We have a ball to get ready for."

He set the drink down and clapped his hands twice. Two guards entered. "Escort the princess to her room."

I didn't fight the guards. I followed them back to the room in a daze. It wasn't until I heard the lock latch behind me that I crumbled to the floor and clutched my stomach. My breaths were short and rapid as I tried to breathe between the sobs that racked my body. Guilt and anger fought for dominance as I lay on the cold floor, not knowing how I would survive. I couldn't let the king hurt anyone else, but I wasn't sure if I could become his obedient little puppet.

CHAPTER 8

Talia

LIGHT PEEKED OUT FROM the curtains, giving false hope of a new day. All I could do throughout the night was recount the impossible situation I was in. There was no way out. I convulsed at the thought. I'd have to find a way to pretend to be the perfect princess who would marry the crown prince. Another shudder broke free at the thought of being married to the King's Wraith.

I couldn't marry him.

I wouldn't.

If I tried to escape again and succeeded, how long would it be before the king sent his men to kill my parents. Because of me.

Vibration from the other side of the door caused me to jump. Distancing myself from the door, I took a deep breath. Another, harder knock followed soon after. Voices whispered to one another, but I couldn't decipher their words.

"Princess Talia, we have your breakfast."

The second I heard Malenee's voice, I hurried to the door, needing to know if Catherine was okay.

"Your Highness." She clutched her chest and gave a bow. But my eyes didn't stay on her for long, because bowing next to her was Catherine.

"What are you doing here?" They both returned my confused expression with ones of their own. "You should be with a Healer or lying down in the least."

"You're too kind, Your Highness, but I'm perfectly fine," Catherine said, with a strained voice. The sweat along her forehead told me all I needed to know about the pain she was enduring.

"That's a lie. You're not okay. You shouldn't be working!"

"Shh." Malenee put her hands up, and they both looked over their shoulders. "Your Highness, may we come in?"

Pinching my eyebrows together, I stepped back to give them access. I didn't say anything until they finished pushing a cart in and had shut the door.

"What's going on?" They refused to look me in the eyes. "I'm going to call for a Healer this second if you don't tell me."

Catherine's face twisted into a grimace as she gave a small nod to Malenee.

"Your Highness, please don't call a Healer. If they find out that Catherine is unfit to work, she will no longer be of use to the king. And...and the king doesn't keep those who are of no use to him."

I shook my head emphatically. "How could he?" I seethed.

"I promise, Your Highness, I can still do my duties." Catherine's eyes were brimming with unshed tears, which turned my anger into guilt.

"Oh, Catherine, I'm so sorry. This is all my fault. If I hadn't tried to escape, you wouldn't have been whipped. Please, forgive me."

"You have nothing to apologize for, Your Highness. I was there. I know you did everything you could to stop it. You even offered yourself." Her eyes shined with gratitude, but her face seemed whiter than normal. "I don't hold you responsible."

Her words did nothing to stop the guilt eating away at my heart.

"Now, what would you like for breakfast?" She carefully turned to face the cart. Malenee and I both inhaled at the same time because dark stains covered her back.

"Go get some hot water and fresh bandages," I ordered Malenee, who thankfully didn't argue.

"Whatever for?" Catherine glanced over her shoulder. The movement caused her to lose her balance. I reached out to catch her as a pained scream erupted from her. She relaxed her weight into my arms, her body shaking from the shock of the pain. Doing what I could to not touch her back, I shuffled her over to my bed and slowly lowered her onto the mattress.

I ran to retrieve a letter opener in the desk to help cut open her uniform. The slender piece of metal wasn't very sharp, so I gave up halfway and used my hands to rip her uniform open.

"Oh. Catherine." Another piece of my heart fell into the bottomless pit of guilt. Under her soaked bandages was puffy, broken flesh. The cuts weren't too deep, so they wouldn't need stitching, as if that made any of it better. I wished for some of Mother's special ointment. It cured everything.

"It's really not that bad, Your Highness," she mumbled against the blanket.

"Yes, it is. Stop lying. I'm a trained Healer."

"Really?"

"Well, I was." My voice dropped. "Once Malenee comes back, I'll apply some fresh bandages and then I order you to rest."

"But—"

"Don't worry. I'll come up with an excuse like needing you to restitch most of my dresses after their stitching broke due to me using them as rope."

A small chuckle escaped her lips, quickly followed by a groan. "Don't make me laugh, Your Highness."

We startled as the door opened, revealing Malenee carrying a bowl and fresh bandages. She deposited the bandages near me, then ran into the washroom to fill the bowl.

Malenee came back with a wet cloth, and I used it to clean Catherine's wounds. With every sharp inhale she took, the anger inside of me grew stronger. I still felt somewhat to blame, but King Madden was fully responsible along with his son. And that was just the beginning. For the rest of my life I would be caged in by their threats.

"Let me help," Malenee said, rolling up her sleeves.

I noticed a mark on her left forearm. It was the King's emblem. The five callings made the points of a star. She quickly placed her arm behind her back, pulling down her sleeve.

"I'll never escape," I whispered, not expecting them to hear me.

"Malenee, tell her," Catherine winced out as I applied some pressure to a deeper gash.

"Tell me what?" I found Malenee's gaze as she prepared the bandages by dipping them in a liquid to help prevent infection.

She drew back her shoulders and released her breath. "Your Highness, we might have a way to help you."

"Help me?"

"It's beyond important that you don't tell anyone what I'm about to tell you." Malenee's eyes widened as she waited for my response.

"I have no one to tell. But I promise."

Nodding her head, she continued, "Have you heard about the Northern Rebels?"

The name sounded familiar, but I couldn't place it. I wrung out the bloody cloth and my memory was jogged. "King Madden accused a young man of being one of them."

"Aiden." She hung her head. "He was one of us."

"Us?"

"Yes. Many servants have recently joined the Northern Rebels ever since one of them infiltrated the King's Guard."

"And this rebel group can help me?"

"Yes. We have been planning a way for you to escape ever since we heard that the king declared you the lost heir. All you have to do is play along with the king's wishes until the ball."

A seed of hope bloomed inside of me, but it quickly wilted.

"I can't escape. He will kill my parents if I do." Dropping my head I placed the cloth in the bloody water and applied the bandages.

"Your Highness, we have people that can protect your family."

"How? They are in Gasmere, and all of you are stuck here in the palace with me."

A smile formed on her lips. "The rebel group is *much* bigger than us. We are all over the kingdom."

"Really?" My eyes widened. "And you're sure they can get to my parents in time?"

"Yes."

I still had some reservations. "Can I ask what the Northern Rebels do?" I placed a bandage with a shrug.

"Right now, we mostly collect intel on the king while waiting for the right time—waiting for you."

"Me?"

"Yes, you," Catherine chimed in with a muffled shout.

"You're the lost princess of Landore. The rightful heir to the throne." Malenee's eyes shined with a promised hope. "We heard rumors that an heir might still be alive, but it was too good to believe. When it became known that King Madden was actively searching for you, we knew it had to be true."

"I'm not anyone special. I don't think this rebel group should expect anything from me," I said, looking down at the last bandage in my hand.

Malenee's hand moved, but she let it fall. "You are. You represent something that Landore is in dire need of."

"What's that?"

"Change."

CHAPTER 9

Raph

"I don't think-k your c-contact is c-coming," Gil stuttered through clenched teeth.

It was the middle of the night, and the salty wind cut straight through my green cloak. I didn't mind though. It helped me stay alert, something all of us needed to be. Gil and Adira crouched next to me with Jules and Eitan on the other side of Adira. The cliffs were the best place to view the palace. However, it was a little hard to communicate with one another over the waves crashing behind us.

We'd spent the past hour scouting out the best escape routes for the night of the ball. Though, what we really needed was some sort of distraction in order to have a clean getaway.

"Raph, did you hear me?" Gil yelled over the wind.

In truth, I had no idea if Tommy had received my message. If he did, I didn't know whether he would risk another meetup. I was about to tell everyone they could head back when Adira tensed beside me.

"You couldn' have picked a warmer spot?" Tommy teased, his voice carrying with the wind.

He and two others stepped out from the denser shadows with their hoods pulled up. I guessed that the other two were Scat and Lemmy, based on their frames. I stood and extended an arm toward him. "Thanks for this," I said, and he gripped my forearm.

"Raphy, you're family. Or have you forgotten?"

He said it jokingly, but it came out a little sharp.

"Never." I tightened my grip before releasing his arm.

"Well, Raphy…" Gil swung his arm over my shoulder as he drawled out the nickname with smug satisfaction. "Are you going to introduce us to your family?"

"Tommy, the leech hanging off me is Gil," I said, then pushed his arm away. "His sister, Adira. And that's Eitan and Jules." Upon me saying their names they nodded their heads, but stayed rigid. "Everyone this is Tommy, Scat, and Lemmy."

The three of them pulled their hoods back, revealing their young faces.

"They're kids." Jules's voice dropped. "I'm not okay with this." She crossed her arms over her chest. I tried to gauge Tommy's reaction, but he seemed unconcerned.

"They're our best shot at a clean getaway. If you aren't okay with it, you don't have to be a part of this. You're free to leave." My words cut through the air like a knife, but I wouldn't take them back. She kept her arms crossed but remained silent.

Adira stepped forward. "What's the plan?" Her eyes hadn't left Scat yet.

"So...you need a clean getaway?" A sly smile pulled at Tommy's lips. "Sounds like you be needin' a distraction."

I shook my head, holding back a smile. "The plan is to sneak into the king's ball."

"Naturally." Tommy gestured for me to continue.

"And to rescue some young women who we think are being held captive in the palace."

"So not only are you tryin' to break into the most guarded place in Landore, but you plan on stealin' somethin' that belongs to the king?"

"Yes," I replied and held my breath. We wouldn't succeed without them.

"We're in." He crossed his arms with a cocky grin. "Been a dream of mine to steal from Ol' Madden. Never thought it'd be people. Eh, works for me." He casually shrugged. But his eyes were ablaze with excitement.

The same look was mirrored in Scat's and Lemmy's faces.

A part of me remembered that feeling of seeing a potential big mark and wanting nothing else but the thrill of going after it.

"Wha' you need?" Tommy asked.

"We have a plan for a way in, but we get stuck at the escape. We have no idea where he is keeping the women. We will need time to look around once we get in. If we do find them, we will need a big enough distraction to get them out."

Tommy rubbed his chin as he stared off into the distance. Lemmy leaned over and whispered in his ear. His eyes lit up in a way that made me nervous. "Oh, we can get you some time."

"Tommy," I said it the way I used to back when it was my job to reign him in.

"Don't you worry 'bout a thin', Raphy."

CHAPTER 10

Talia

"WHO ARE YOU REQUIRED to formally greet?" Celeste asked as she paced behind me.

It had been four days since my attempted escape, and since then, every day had been spent the same way, with Celeste pounding etiquette lessons into my head.

"I am to bow to the king, and then the prince because the prince is the heir. If he wasn't, we would have the same rank, and I wouldn't be required to," I answered, sitting tall next to the warm fire. It was the one thing I had requested from Malenee and Catherine, that a fire constantly be lit. The smokey smell brought me a piece of comfort. Celeste didn't approve, which made it that much better.

"Correct." Her voice was anything but pleased.

I glanced out the far window where the frozen rain beat against the glass, hoping all the training would be worth it in the end.

"If a duke engages you in conversation, what topics must you adhere to?"

"The weather, the health of their family, and any nonpolitical interests they may have like hunting, horses, archery, and gardening." Or ideally, not say anything at all, I thought with an eye roll.

"Is everything alright, Princess?" She popped the P on the title, challenging me to mess up.

My fists tightened around my fine silk skirt, most likely ruining it. But each time she called me princess, it felt like tying another rock to my heart, reminding me of my father, my real father, lovingly calling me that. She knew it had an effect on me.

"Yes, everything is perfect," I answered, mimicking her popped P.

The past four days had also consisted of Celeste trying to find a weak spot to try and exploit, so she could report it to the king. I refused to let her win. I had something much stronger than her hate toward me. I had hope. Hope that, in a matter of days, I'd escape it all.

A knock echoed through the room breaking our silent stare-off.

"Come in," I said. I knew exactly who was behind the door. Because I only ever saw the same people, and I was never allowed out of the room.

"We have the reading material you requested, Lady Celeste." Mistress Pennier entered, her arms empty as Malenee and Catherine followed her each carrying a stack of books. They placed the books on the already overflowing desk before they retreated to the edge of the room.

"Where do you keep getting these books?"

"The king's library, Your Highness," Celeste answered in her sweet, musical voice.

"I would love to see it."

"There is no need—"

"That could be arranged, Your Highness," Mistress Pennier cut her off. "I'll present your request to the king. Based on how well your training has gone, I'm sure he'll accept."

"Thank you." I gave her a full smile. I hadn't figured out Mistress Pennier yet. She was the etiquette governess over the noble women, and clearly favored Celeste, but there were moments when I didn't dislike her that much.

"Of course." She bowed. "I'll let you get back to your training."

After she shut the door, I looked back over to the desk where Celeste was standing with her arms crossed and a look that could kill.

"Lady Celeste, is there a problem?"

She stayed unmoving. I almost got worried until she released her arms in a huff and transformed her face back to her fake smile.

"No, Your Highness. Let's begin." She gestured to the desk.

I sat behind the tall stack of books and reached for the leather-bound one on top. The earthy smell I had become accustomed to engulfed me as I opened the book to the first marked page. Most of the books she had me read from seemed fairly new, but that one appeared older. The pages were discolored, worn, and almost brittle to the touch.

I cleared my throat and read out loud. Celeste went to sit in front of me, picking up the same piece of fabric she had been working on earlier. My reading had improved enough that she no longer hovered over my shoulder.

I moved my gaze to Malenee and Catherine for a brief second, wishing I could demand they sit down. Catherine's wounds were healing nicely, but all they did throughout the day was stand next to the wall or clean. Malenee's eyes met mine, urging me to start reading again. Taking a deep breath, I turned the page and read—for what felt like hours.

"That's enough. Close the book, Your Highness," Celeste ordered. I waited as she neatly placed her hands in her lap. "What kingdom traded in tin and lead?"

"Vasdere," I stated confidently. I hated to admit it, but I was enjoying learning so much about the other three kingdoms.

"What about the Kingdom of Tro'ish?"

"Its mountainous terrain produced commodities for trading, like gemstones and other minerals." I gave a nod of my head, feeling good about my answer.

"Correct. Is there anything else you can tell me about the Kingdom?" Celeste raised her eyebrows. It was her favorite time of the day, testing me until I undoubtedly gave a wrong answer.

"It is also the one kingdom that had the least amount of contact with the other kingdoms."

"Yes. Where is it located?"

"It is on the eastern side?" I said, scrunching up my face. Celeste's bright smile told me that I was wrong.

"Western. The Kingdom of Nefali and Vasdere are on the eastern side of Landore," she explained with a shake of her head.

"It would be easier if there was a map," I muttered.

"Tell me about the Kingdom of Nefali."

"It's located above Vasdere on the eastern side of Landore," I said with emphasis. "They traded in various spices and silks."

"And?" She leaned forward.

"They are believed to have murdered the late royal family," I recited, unconvinced it was really them. Especially after realizing that Nadav and Hafsa were most likely from there. But based on how they always covered themselves and how people reacted to them, it made sense that people believed it to be true. "It doesn't make sense."

"What doesn't."

"The four kingdoms had peace for one hundred years. Why would one of them suddenly destroy it?"

"It doesn't have to make sense, Princess. That is what happened." Her voice was sharp, but I couldn't let it go. The frustration about being kept in the dark about so many things was boiling over.

"So you believe the Kingdom of Nefali broke ties with its biggest trading resource on purpose?"

"Yes. That is what the book says, and that is what the king says. You need to stop questioning things and believe what you're told." Her voice raised an octave.

"Do you understand how messed up that sounds?" From the corner of my eyes, I saw Catherine and Malenee's posture go rigid.

"Stop!" She threw her arms in the air. "It shouldn't be you. You aren't fit to be Landore's future queen. It was supposed to be me!" Her face flushed, and a single tear made its way down her cheek.

I opened my mouth to say something, but nothing came out.

"Excuse me, Your Highness," she said, rising to her feet. "That is all for today." She gave a quick bow before exiting the room at almost a run, that still looked graceful. When the door closed, I looked at Catherine and Malenee, but they had the same expression of shock on their faces.

I finally understood how they were able to keep bringing me stack after stack of books. There must have been thousands of books in one section of the room alone. I couldn't get my mouth to stay closed as the cataloger led me and Mistress Pennier around the next corner, opening to a black spiral staircase.

"Up there contains the books regarding the four kingdoms prior to the hundred years of peace," the cataloger said.

"How far back do they go?" I asked, straining my neck to see how far back the rows of bookshelves went.

"All the way to the founding of the four kingdoms to when the four Albeit brothers each ruled a kingdom." He pushed up his bifocals.

"The who?"

"Don't worry about that now, Your Highness," Mistress Pennier chimed in. "You will have your whole life to uncover all the knowledge these books hold."

"It would take more than one lifetime, Mistress Pennier. There is a reason why Landore was known as the kingdom of wisdom," the cataloger corrected.

"Really?" I asked. Everything the cataloger was saying felt like it was about another kingdom.

"Oh, yes, Your Highness." He bowed his head, which caused him to have to fix his bifocals again. He opened his mouth to speak more on the subject, but Mistress Pennier cut in.

"Thank you, Alfred, for the tour. But let's leave Her Highness alone. She only has a small time allotted tonight to browse these wonderful books."

"Yes, of course, Mistress Pennier." He shuffled backward. "Take as many as you'd like, Your Highness."

"If you need anything just call. There are guards posted all around." Mistress Pennier followed Alfred back toward the front of the room.

I gazed up to the tops of the bookshelves that were at least twice my height. I was still in shock that these books existed and hadn't been destroyed. Running my hand along the dark, mahogany wood of the shelves, I took my time walking in and out of the different aisles, allowing myself to get completely lost. For a moment, I felt free, like I wasn't pretending to be anything. My hand moved up the spines of the books as I read the different titles.

"Herbal Remedies," I whispered, pulling the book from the shelf. I opened it to the first page. It read, A Healer's Chronicle of Annual Herbs. My heart ached. Mother would love that book. Shoving it back on the shelf, I hurried to the end of the aisle.

Thump.

I peered back to see a book on the ground, where I had just been.

Retracing my steps, I picked it up and looked for where it came from. But it wasn't like any of the other books in that area. It was much thinner, and there wasn't a title on it. Flipping through the pages, I saw sloppy handwriting that had some sort of timestamp at the top of the page. Turning back to the first page, I began to read.

Early Spring

Father says I have no choice in the matter. To ensure our kingdom's safety we must align with Landore. That will be the solution to protect us from any foul plans Tro'ish has. He says the rumors are growing stronger and that they have plans to conquer us. If we align with Landore, our kingdom would be protected by their army as well. It is my duty as the princess of Vasdere, but how am I supposed to marry someone I have never met before.

He is handsome, at least from the portrait one of their advisers brought with them, but is he kind, generous, respectful? Could I love him?

"Princess Talia," a guard's voice called out. I jolted and lost hold of the book. Quickly picking it up, I grabbed a couple of other random books on the shelf, hiding the book between them. The guard rounded the corner.

"Your Highness, your time is up," he said with a bow.

"Coming."

"Would you like me to carry those for you?"

"No! I would prefer to do it myself, thank you."

His brow hitched, but he didn't say anything else. He led me to the front of the room where Mistress Pennier was no longer anywhere in sight. Instead, lounging in a chair next to the door was Prince Kasper.

I back stepped as his sharp, gray eyes found me. He instantly stood and approached.

"I'll take it from here, Gideon," Prince Kasper said to the guard while standing slightly in front of me.

"Of course, Your Highness."

"Shall we go?" he asked nonchalantly.

"Go where?" my voice shook with a mix of anger and fear.

"To your room. I'm here to escort you back."

My heart rate evened out slightly at knowing he wasn't taking me to see the king. I nodded and stepped to the side, trying to put distance between us.

"Let me hold those." He reached out as I pulled the books closer to my chest.

"Never mind," he said, holding his hands up with a curious look in his eye. "After you." He gestured forward.

I stepped out in front of him, but I realized I didn't know my way back, so I slowed my steps and allowed him to walk next to me.

"Did you find what you were looking for?" He asked with a hint of laughter in his voice.

"Yes."

"You know, at the ball, it will be expected for us to carry on a conversation."

"Fine." Stopping, I turned to face him. "How?"

"How must we converse with each other?"

"No. How could you kidnap those young women? How could you whip Catherine? How can you go along with doing such awful things?" My face was hot, and my chest was tight.

His eyes widened, and for a moment, his face almost looked pained, but it morphed into anger. "Because I'm the King's Wraith." He turned on his heel and continued down the hall.

Clutching the books tighter, I followed.

CHAPTER 11

Jules

"Jules. Jules."

Hands wrapped around my shoulders, shaking me awake. I bolted upright and pushed myself into the corner of the wall.

"It's okay. It's me." I focused on Adira's bright hair and golden eyes. She stood next to my bed with her arms in front of her. "I'm not going to hurt you."

I pushed my wet hair off my face and breathed deeply. I wrapped my arms around my knees, trying to stop my body from shaking.

"You were screaming." Adira watched my every twitch.

"I know. I'm sorry." I dropped my forehead onto my knees.

The bed dipped as Adira sat on the edge. "Want to talk about it?"

"Not really."

"Do you want to get out of here?"

She was fully dressed. "Where were you going?"

"I couldn't sleep. Thought I'd go put eyes on the palace. Want to come?"

"Yes," I said, then I pushed myself away from the wall. The past three days had been unbearable as we counted down the days to the ball. I grabbed my bow and quiver, and instantly felt better.

The creaking of the stairs was the only thing that could be heard as we made our way downstairs. There was a faint light coming from under the door where the kitchen was, but other than that, it was vacant. We exited the Lucky Lion without saying a word and entered the cool of the night. The wind howled like a pack of wolves, cutting through my cloak with no sympathy.

Our tavern was on the far northwest side of Llycia. It would take us a good hour before we got to the palace. The homes and shops in the area were closed and dark. We saw no one on the streets except for the occasional rat that would scamper by.

"Have you had those dreams ever since..." Adira asked, grabbing the sides of her hood so it wouldn't blow off.

I dipped my head. "Yeah."

"You were screaming out for someone called Suz?"

"She was one of the women who was kidnapped with me," I explained, but not sharing how each night the woman in my dream changed. Everything else stayed the same: a man covered in shadows would stalk toward them, and they would cry out for me to help. I was always tied to a tree, unable to do anything as I watched him beat them. "They will stop," I said, wrapping my arms around my waist, "once we rescue Tals."

Adira glanced at me. Her mouth opened, but she shut it again without saying a word. We continued on, saying nothing.

"Woah," a man slurred as he almost knocked into me when he stumbled out of a tavern.

"Trev, where you going?" Another man stepped out of the tavern and grabbed the drunk man's arm, pulling him away from us. Their zig-zagged steps took them across the street. We saw a few other people shuffle their way down the streets, finally calling it a night.

"What about you guys?" I asked as we made the turn onto the paved street that led to the palace. Adira didn't acknowledge my question, so I continued, "Tals might have been okay with the secrecy, but I'm not as accepting."

She finally glanced my way with a single raised brow at me.

"Who are you guys, really? Where are you from?"

"Why does it matter? What could I say that would stop you from joining us to save Talia?"

I pressed my lips together.

"All you need to know is that we want what's best for Landore and its people. We are willing to do a lot to ensure that."

"Are there more like you guys?"

She gave out a small laugh. "You two are a lot alike, you know that?"

"We are best friends."

"Must be nice." Her voice lowered.

It was my turn to raise an eyebrow.

Exhaling, she answered, "I've never had many friends. I especially never had a friendship like you and Talia."

"What about Eitan and Raph?"

"Hah, I've been stuck with those two for six years. They are more like brothers than friends."

I shook my head, understanding.

"It wasn't until Talia joined our group that I really felt like I could have a friend."

"She has that way about her."

"Yeah."

The sound of horse hooves and wheels rolling on the stoned street made us both turn around. A wagon was flying up the street behind us. We moved to the side, but there was a group of drunk Hunters singing loudly and off key in the middle of the road.

"Move!" The man driving the wagon shouted at the oblivious group. His shouts were lost in the wind. "Get out of the way!" For some reason, he refused to slow down.

Adira and I both looked at each other, then we sprinted toward them, shouting along the way. It wasn't until we were almost ten feet in front of them that one of them noticed us. Their off-tune song grew louder as the drunk man waved at us to join them. We frantically threw our arms in the air, gesturing to the approaching wagon. His head turned, and everything seemed to happen in slow motion. He pushed his friends out of the way, right before the wagon flashed by, causing Adira and me to jump back so we didn't get run over.

I pressed my hand against my heaving chest to control my breathing. The group moved on, barely phased. "Why didn't he stop?"

"Great question." Her eyes narrowed in the direction the wagon had gone. "Want to find out?" The side of her mouth lifted.

I replied with a smirk of my own.

The wagon was out of sight, but we could still hear the horse hooves. The sound led us straight to the palace gates.

"Interesting." Adira breathed as we ducked behind a nearby tree.

"Can you see them?" I whispered.

"No," she said, throwing her head up.

Adira jumped into the air and gripped the lowest branch, pulling herself effortlessly onto the branch. "You got it?"

"Sure."

I backed up, thinking a running start might help, because Adira had about five inches on me. Taking a slow inhale, I sprang forward. Bending my knees, I pushed into the ground. My fingertips skimmed the branch, but my feet didn't return to the ground. Adira's hands were wrapped around my wrists. I grabbed the branch, and she scooted back so I could swing a leg up.

"Thanks," I breathed.

"No problem."

We climbed higher until we could get a good look over the palace wall. An orange glow broke through the horizon, giving us enough light to see the wagon sitting in front of the palace doors. The driver jumped down and walked to the back, unlocking the door. Two other men, almost twice the driver's size, came out. My eyes wouldn't leave one of them. His whole head was shaved, but there were strange colorful markings on it.

A gust of wind shook the branches, and I had to grab onto the tree to not fall. I looked back and the two men each carried a box to the palace steps where two guards stood. No words seemed to be exchanged as the guards took the boxes and walked up the palace steps.

The three men returned to their wagon. Not much later, the palace gate opened again, and they left.

"What do you think that was about?" I asked.

"No clue."

"Should we tell Raph?"

"We will when he and Gil get back," she said, then she threw herself from the tree and landed in a perfect crouch.

"They are not normal." I shook my head before climbing down to the lowest branch and jumped off.

CHAPTER 12

Raph

"WHY COULDN'T YOU HAVE taken Eitan with you for this," Gil complained as he wrapped his cloak tighter around himself. Another strong gust of sleet slammed into us as we walked on the wooden pier along the docks. The beginning of winter was never forgiving in Llycia, it always heralded its coming with a vengeance.

"You wanted to get out of the tavern. Here you go," I replied while pushing my damp hair back. Truthfully, I would rather have handled it on my own, but we were all getting tired of Gil's constant complaining. At least coming with me would shut him up for a while.

"Why are we down here? Every other sensible person has vacated the area. This weather is unbearable," he muttered.

The weather was especially ugly, but with the ball being the next night, we had to go to that area. Nowhere else had the supplies we needed because, even on nice days, only a certain crowd visited the docks. Since no boats were ever allowed in or out, that part of Llycia was deserted and rundown.

"Raph, are we close?"

"Yes. It's right over—"

A small yellow ribbon, tied to one of the shop's broken windowsills, danced in the wind. My heart stopped for a moment. The same fear I'd felt as a Shade whenever I saw a yellow ribbon rushed back. Blue meant a meeting was needed; green was it's safe; brown was be cautious; and yellow meant hide. Yellow meant poachers were out, and they were the Shades' biggest threat—not the King's Guard or the King's Wraith.

Instinctively, I scoured the area for somewhere safe to hole up in. Gil placed his hand on my shoulder, and I reflexively moved away.

"Hey, is everything alright?"

"Yeah, I'm fine." Looking at Gil reminded me that I was no longer a defenseless street orphan. A poacher wouldn't look twice at me now. "You sure? You look like you are about to hurl. I don't want to be near you if that is what's going to happen next." Gil took a step away, but he couldn't hide his smirk.

"I'm fine."

"Great. I can't believe I'm going to say this but let's hurry up and get what we need so we can get back to the Lucky Lion." Gil shook his head, and we continued toward the deteriorating shops. I had to give the door a few shoves before it cracked open. The wind whistled through the gap as I pried it wide enough for a body to fit.

"I don't think this is much better than outside," Gil whispered behind me.

My eyes roamed the familiar shop, if you could call it that. The room we stood in looked like an average sitting room of any house, if it had been abandoned for years. It smelled of damp wood and rot. There were a few chairs surrounding an uneven table, a ripped sofa next to a dying fire, and one closed door leading to another room.

"I think I'm going to wait for you outside."

"Scared?" I taunted while making my way over to the fireplace, noticing Gil rooted to the same spot by the door.

"No," he said defiantly. "I would rather take my chances with the wind than with whoever lives in all of...this." He threw his arms out, gesturing to the whole room.

Shaking my head, I reached on top of the mantle where there still sat a black wooden crow with red beady eyes. I felt underneath its boxed stand and grazed a cool piece of metal with the tips of my fingers.

"Nothing's changed," I whispered under my breath.

"What'd you say?"

SNAP!

I turned and saw Gil standing over the newly broken table with his hands in the air.

"I hardly touched it!"

"Let's go." I moved toward the closed door, pushed the key into the lock, and turned it until I heard a click. Gil gasped as I opened the door into the real shop.

Candlelight illuminated a narrow hallway revealing different people wearing an array of colors, all from different callings, walking in and out of different rooms.

I took a step forward, but Gil's hand clamped down on my shoulder. "Where are we?"

"I told you. We're in a shop for supplies." I rolled my shoulder, bumping his hand off.

"*This* is the shop?"

"Yes. Come on."

I passed by the first room to my right without a glance. What we needed wasn't going to be found out in the open. The strong smell of perfumes and spices told me exactly what could be found in that first room. I continued down the hallway until I no longer heard Gil's steps behind me. I spotted his blond locks going into the last door on the left. Groaning, I retraced my steps back.

"Of course, this would be the room you couldn't resist going in." I stopped beside him.

"What is this place?" he asked, his eyes devouring the rare gems in front of him.

I looked around, remembering how, as a kid, I had spent a lot of time in these rooms looking at the exotic goods that came in from the other kingdoms. I'd pretend I was a great adventurer who traveled to faraway lands.

"What are these?" Gil reached toward the stones.

"Y'a break, y'a buy." A woman's voice resounded in the room.

Gil and I turned to watch a plump, old woman hobble toward us using a wooden cane.

"Y'a wouldn't happen to be the one who broke my table out front, would y'a?" Her wrinkled face lifted as she gave us an accusatory stare. She was within striking distance of us with her cane.

"That thing is older than you, Stella. It would have collapsed after another layer of dust, and you know it," I teased, pulling my hood down and throwing her a rare smile.

"Well, well, well…" Her raspy voice hit me with a wave of forgotten memories. She was the closest thing to a mother for us Shades. "Tommy wasn't lying when he said little Raphy had made his way back home." She returned my smile with one of her own, one that was missing a few more teeth since the last time I saw it. "Don't get me wrong. It's good to see y'a alive and in person, Raphy. But what are y'a doing back? And why are y'a involving Tommy? He gets into too much trouble as it is." She shook her cane violently, causing Gil to take a step back.

"I know. Trust me, I wouldn't be here if I had another choice." I had tried to acquire what we needed on my own and had failed.

"So what are y'a needing from Old Aunt Stella this time?"

"You own this shop?" Gil asked, leaving his mouth open.

"The day that man closed the borders was the day I opened up shop. He has made me quite a wealthy woman," she finished with a wink.

Gil took in the other rare gems and sculptures scattered throughout the room. "Where do you get everything?"

"Ah, that there is a secret I will take to my grave. Now, hurry up, spit it out. What y'a needing? I'm a busy woman, and my time is valuable."

Stepping closer, I lowered my voice. "We need four servant uniforms."

"Boy, that better not be the only thing y'a needing. Y'a can find those in any one of the shops in town."

"Stella," I said with some steel, "we need to look like servants that will be working the ball."

Understanding dawned on her face before she gave a disapproving stare. "Does this also have to do with why Tommy requested some very expensive and dangerous materials from me? What do y'a have planned?" She might have aged since the last time I saw her, but she still carried that same fight.

"I promise, nothing will happen to Tommy."

"Hmmm..." She looked me over for a good minute. "This will cost y'a."

"I know."

"And I'm talking about real money, not those bits of information y'a Shades like to tempt me with."

"Name your price." I took the sack of coins I kept around my neck off.

Before I had time to react, her wrinkled hand snatched the sack from my grasp. "This will do," she said, weighing the sack in her palm.

"You're getting a little rusty," Gil snickered at me.

"Who do y'a think taught him how to survive on those cursed streets?" she chided, tucking the sack of coins under her apron. "I'll have what y'a need tomorrow morning. Now be gone before you break something else of mine."

I turned to leave but stopped in the doorframe. "It's good to see you, Stella."

"Y'a too, Raphy. Now go before I charge y'a for that table."

The wind was still going strong as we closed the weathered door behind us. The sun was halfway down the horizon as we started on our way back to the tavern. I tried to keep my eyes focused ahead, but I couldn't stop myself from finding that yellow ribbon we had passed by. I stared at it, and it was almost like I could hear her screams. The same screams that haunted me every night. As we left the line of shops, the screams seemed to get louder. I halted.

"Do you hear that?" I asked Gil.

"Huh?"

"Do you hear that screaming?"

"The wind hasn't stopped screaming since we stepped onto this forsaken pier."

"No. Gil, listen." I urged, closing my eyes.

"Is that...a child?"

CHAPTER 13

Raph

I DIDN'T HEAR THE rest of what Gil said because my feet were already pounding against the ground. I prayed that I was wrong, that it was the wind playing tricks on me, but I couldn't chance it.

I needed to move faster. The screams were coming from the other end of the shops. And the closer I got the more defined they became.

"Help! Somebody, help me!"

I was close. But the next scream was muffled, so I pushed harder, unwilling to let the poachers take another one.

Suddenly, they stopped. I turned and sprinted down a narrow alley. At the far end, two large men struggled to hold on to a small child who kept thrashing.

My blood warmed as rage coursed through me. I withdrew two daggers and looked for a clear shot. It was dark in the alley, and I wouldn't risk hitting a kid. As they lifted the kid into a crate, I pushed off my heels and sprinted.

The man carrying the kid's upper body was the first to see me, but the one facing away must have heard me because he whipped his head over his shoulder. The kid's eyes locked with mine. It was Scat.

His head was covered with blood, and it streamed down his face. A rag was tied around his mouth, which explained the muffled screams. Relief took over his face when he recognized me until the men dropped him into the crate.

Midrun I flung a dagger straight into the hand of the large man furthest away and another right after into the other's thigh. The lid of the crate fell to the floor, and at the same time I made contact with the one who had my dagger protruding from his leg. He was slow to react to my movement, and my right cross hit him square in the jaw. He staggered back favoring his leg. He had a similar frame to Eitan, but I could tell he only ever used his brute strength to fight. I was able to get a couple more hits in before he landed his first blow to my face. Hot pain radiated throughout my jaw, but it gave me the opening I was looking for. I delivered two strikes under his jaw and followed them up with a kick straight to my blade that was still lodged in his thigh. A guttural cry erupted as the blade tore through his flesh. But before I could finish him, the slightly smaller man, with a bald head covered in markings, approached. Blood dripped down his hand from where my blade had been lodged.

Taking a few steps back, I assessed them both. Every part of me knew I could take them. For seven years, Alon had trained me into an elite warrior. Fighting them would be nothing.

They came at me at once, but their moves were sluggish and predictable. Every hit I landed, I pictured one of those innocent faces and exacted revenge for every child they had taken. At one point, red was the only thing that flooded my vision. The sound of something scraping the ground cleared my mind.

There was another one.

He was dragging a now unconscious Scat out of the alley, making a left.

Where was Gil?

I deflected their swings, knowing they were tiring and about two good hits away from being knocked out. If I went after Scat who knew if they would still be around by the time I got back. And the thought of losing them and the information they had, made me hesitate. But then *her* face came into my mind. I delivered a side kick to the bald man and gave an uppercut to the other one, then sprinted after Scat.

Coughs racked my body as a gust of wind hit me. For a moment, I couldn't see anything but the barren streets near the docks. They couldn't have gone far. I was only a few seconds behind them.

Movement from the corner of my eye made me move across the street and to the right where a horse and wagon were waiting. Scat was lying on the ground while the man opened the back door.

But before I approached, the sound of running had me turning around to find a breathless Gil. I pointed to Scat lying on the ground, and Gil nodded in response.

Slamming the door closed, I met the poacher's surprised face with a right hook to his jaw. He stumbled back, holding what, I assumed, was his now dislocated jaw. He was a lot smaller than the other two, certainly not the muscle of the group. As he watched me approach, his eyes grew with fear, and he bolted.

Tightening my fists, I released an annoyed groan and turned to head after him.

"Raph," Gil's voice called out, etched with concern.

I glanced back to see his hands covered in blood.

CHAPTER 14

Talia

"YOUR HIGHNESS, PLEASE HOLD still," the grumpy seamstress ordered as another needle in her hand poked me in the side. For some reason, my last few dress fittings hadn't been enough.

When I had complained at the last one, Celeste chastised me about how grateful I should be, for the seamstress was the best dressmaker in all of Llycia and only the wealthiest could afford her services. I didn't care about any of it. It was a waste of money and fabric. In Gasmere, the majority of women borrowed dresses from each other for special occasions, not have one made. I tried, and failed, at getting them to let me wear one of the countless dresses they had already made for me.

"Ouch," I yelped as another needle jabbed me in the side. She had to take the dress in again. I tried to eat, but at this point, I would wither away before King Madden had the chance to marry me off.

"If you'd hold still, I'd be finished already," she grumbled.

But after standing for two hours, I couldn't stop my legs from shaking. The only good thing was that my training with Celeste got canceled that day. I wasn't told why, but I had a feeling it had to do with her confession because I hadn't seen her since. I planned to spend my free evening reading that journal.

"There, done. I will finish the rest at my shop and have it sent back in plenty of time." She said the last part to Malenee and Catherine, who had reentered the room with an assortment of pastries. The dressmaker turned back to me. "Don't suddenly gain an appetite now, Your Highness. There is no more time to do more altering." Her stare was unrelenting. It felt like I was being scolded by an Elder.

I nodded my head, and with that, she took her leave.

"Your Highness, we've put out some pastries for you." Catherine's hand shook slightly as she placed a plate filled with baked goods on the table.

"How are you feeling?" I asked.

"All better..." she hesitated at seeing my determined face. "It gets better each day, Your Highness. Thank you."

"Please, eat something, Your Highness," Malenee implored. "You need to build your strength for tomorrow night. You'll be on your feet dancing for the majority of it."

"We can't have the Princess of Landore fainting at her own ball." Catherine giggled.

The smell of fresh bread and sugar overwhelmed me. My mouth watered, but I knew what would happen after I took a bite. I sat, grabbed the pastry in front of me, and took a bite. At first, the sweet flavor of fig and nutmeg filled my mouth, but that sweetness quickly turned into ash and formed a solid lump in my stomach. Out of the corner of my eye, I saw both Catherine and Malenee relax their shoulders as I swallowed.

"Have you heard any updates?" My legs bounced underneath the table.

Malenee gave me a soft smile. "Word was sent this morning. Someone is on their way to Gasmere to retrieve your parents, and also, your friend, Jules, and her family."

The heavy weight encasing my heart lightened, but my legs kept shaking. I set the pastry down without taking another bite. "Good, that's good."

"It will work out, Your Highness." Catherine placed another pastry on my plate. "You don't have to worry."

"Your job is to act like everything is normal. When the time comes, someone will find you." Malenee came to stand next to Catherine.

"Now, tell us more about this journal you found." Catherine clapped her hands together with an excited smile. "I'm dying to know if she marries the prince and what he's like." Her eyes glossed over as she stared off into the distance.

Malenee shook her head. "I wonder who the journal belonged to." She placed her hand under her chin. "Your Highness, you said there are no dates written anywhere, just the seasons, right?"

"I haven't seen any, but I haven't been able to read every page."

"Have you learned anything new?" Catherine's eager eyes latched onto me.

"Yes, a little," I said, releasing a small laugh. "The princess is on her way to Landore, and she is not a fan of traveling by ship."

"That's it?" Catherine said with a drop of her chin.

"If I wasn't kept busy every moment of the day, I would have more time to read."

Catherine was the first to smile, then me, and last Malenee gave a small upward lift of her right lip.

"I did find out, however, after scouring the library, that the names of the late king and queen were Davis and Aleese."

Both of their eyes widened.

"Your Highness, King Madden doesn't allow their names to be spoken," Malenee said, looking around the room.

In Gasmere, no one spoke about the late royal family, it was deemed irrelevant. "Why?" I asked.

Knock. Knock.

We froze.

Malenee opened the door, only to close it again. She walked back with a small piece of parchment in her hand.

"It's for you, Your Highness, from the king." She handed the note to me slowly.

I unfolded it with sweaty hands and read its contents.

Little Fawn,

I desire an audience with you. You will take part in a family dinner, tonight.

The words blurred together as my hands trembled.

"Your Highness, are you okay?" Catherine's voice was muffled over the erratic pounding of my heart.

"He knows," I said, returning the note back to Malenee. "He knows something. This can't be good." I lifted my hand to my neck and paced the room, then I moved it back down to my side.

"Relax, Your Highness. You don't know that." Malenee handed the note to Catherine. "Knowing the king, he probably wants to ensure you can behave like a princess. He will want to give his approval before the ball."

"That makes sense." I stopped. "What if he has found out about our plans?"

"He hasn't," Malenee assured, placing her hand on my shoulder, and just as quickly, she retracted it, seeming to have remembered her place. And mine.

"Your Highness, we made sure nothing would lead back to you. You're safe." A grim smile covered Catherine's face at her last words. We knew I would never be safe around the king.

"We should get you ready, Your Highness," Malenee stated from behind me.

They were quick. Before I realized it, my hair and makeup were completed, and I stood dressed in a full-skirted gown.

"I'll notify the guard, Your Highness." At my nod, Malenee walked over to the door.

Needing a distraction, I walked over to one of the large windows overlooking the ocean. I never imagined I'd see the ocean. I never imagined leaving Gasmere, but so much had happened in the past month.

The wind matched my inner turmoil, howling outside the window, causing the waves to slap against the black rocks. I wished to be able to go out and put my feet in the frigid water, to walk along the black beach, and to listen to the sounds of the ocean up close. It called to me, yearning for me to come into its waters and be washed away.

"Have you been in the ocean?" I asked Catherine, curious about what those powerful waves against my body would feel like.

"Of course." Catherine walked over to join me at the window. "But never in the winter." She shivered as if she could feel the cold water upon her skin.

"I don't know how to swim."

"I didn't either before I came to the palace."

"How *did* you come to be here?" I asked cautiously.

Her shoulders raised as she held her breath.

"You don't have to answer."

Her lips moved as she released the tension in her shoulders. "You are too generous, Your Highness. My story is not that different from many others who serve in the palace."

I contemplated how to reply, not wanting the door she opened to close. "How many years have you been a maid for?" I asked.

"Thirteen."

"Thirteen years? That means you must have been like six or something."

"Five. I was tak—brought here when I was five." Her eyes grew wide.

I pulled back at her response. How could they take a five-year-old girl from her family?

"What about your fam—"

"A guard is here to escort you, Your Highness," Malenee declared from the door.

Catherine's lips tightened as she bowed her head. Reluctantly, I made my way to the door. Malenee gave me a reassuring smile when I passed by her to follow the guard down the hall.

CHAPTER 15

Talia

I SHOOK MY HEAD at the sight of the room the guard left me alone in. I don't know why I was surprised by the mere size of it. So far every room I'd seen was enormous. It felt bare and cold. The tapestries should have helped, but they were depictions of animals being hunted and slaughtered. A shiver rocked through me when I accidentally made eye contact with one of the many animal heads displayed on the walls. Averting my gaze, I went to the long table in the middle of the room and sat to the left of the head of the table, remembering Celeste's teaching.

At the sound of the door opening, I stood from my chair, almost tipping it over in my hurry. Prince Kasper paused in the doorway. "Should have guessed you were the reason for this dinner." His voice was low. I couldn't decipher whether he was mad, disappointed, or curious.

He took long strides into the room, ignoring the small bow I was taught to give. He dropped into a seat across from me. Some of the tension in me eased, but the unbreakable silence that followed made the room stuffy. I stared at the dark table, not wanting to meet his eye.

The door opened again, and I sprang to my feet, noticing that Prince Kasper took his time standing. King Madden stormed into the room and awaited our bows before he sat at the head of the table.

"Move," he barked at his son. "Sit next to your soon-to-be wife. I want to see you two together. This is as much of a test for you as her."

King Madden's gaze moved to me, and for a moment, he had a far-off look in his eyes before it switched to analyzing my appearance. Prince Kasper moved to sit next to me, but the king's gaze didn't waver once. "You look the part." He gestured at the burgundy dress I wore. It was the heaviest dress I had ever worn. It was composed of five skirts on top of each other, creating a large tent underneath me. The bodice's tight fit made it nearly impossible for me to slouch. I had a feeling that it would grow increasingly uncomfortable as the dinner progressed.

"I guess the real question is, what will happen when you open that little mouth of yours?" King Madden remarked. I pressed my lips together from the fear of saying or doing the wrong thing. "Go ahead." He waved his hand. "Speak freely. I need to know what you will say unbridled."

Before I could determine what to say, two young women entered carrying large, covered trays. I seized the opportunity to avoid King Madden's harsh gaze and studied them as they laid out the meal. They seemed to be around my age and were extremely skittish. They bowed and scurried out of the room like scared animals. My focus was drawn back to the animals on the wall behind the king as I wished I could run from the room too.

"Do you enjoy my trophies?" he asked, cutting into the meat on his plate. His smile was predatorial.

I squeezed my hands under the table to stop them from shaking as I drew air into my lungs. "What did you do with the other women?" I asked. My conversation with Catherine earlier and seeing those maids had me thinking the worst. I tried to ask what had become of the other women who were in the throne room with me, but every time I attempted it, everyone immediately changed the subject or found something new to do.

He studied me over his wine glass. He gave a wicked smile as he placed his drink down. "You may have your grandmother's fighting spirit in you, but hopefully, you have more wisdom than your grandfather." He shook his head and reached for the glass. "They are where they are meant to be," he replied finally.

"Are they safe? Were they taken back home?" Any composure I had been trying to maintain was instantly destroyed.

The king took a slow bite of his food. "Little Fawn," he chided, "tomorrow night, you will be presented as the lost princess of Landore. I don't need to remind you of the many lives that hang in the balance as a result of how well you sell that, do I?" He gave a pointed look, similar to a disapproving father to their disobedient child. "You shouldn't worry your pretty little head about a few young women." He paused to drink from the glass in front of him. "You just make sure your performance at the ball is a success." He punctuated his explanation by taking a bite of his food.

My stomach turned, and I pushed the food around my plate feigning interest. How could he expect me to be the perfect princess after six days?

"I will do my best," I vowed with a shaky voice.

"That is not good enough," he seethed. "Starting tomorrow night, you represent me. Everything you say or do reflects upon me. I demand perfection and absolute obedience. I will not have people think I'm weak because of you." His eyes drilled into me as his face darkened.

I lowered my head.

He picked his silverware back up and cut into the large piece of meat on his plate.

"That won't be all. You two," he said, pointing the knife between the prince and me, "must make the people believe you can do more than tolerate each other. The people become more malleable when love is involved."

Prince Kasper pressed his back against the chair while I choked on my saliva.

"The sooner you warm up to each other, the better. After the ball, your engagement will be out to the public. You will need to be seen together at parties hosted by my court, showing the people you are in love."

I looked to Kasper, hoping he would say something to oppose his father, but all he did was stare at his food. He truly was an obedient pet. I reminded myself that it didn't matter because, after the ball, I wouldn't be under the king's control anymore, and I wouldn't have to pretend to be in love with Prince Kasper because I wouldn't be marrying him.

Thankfully, King Madden didn't say or demand anything else as he consumed the rest of his food. After his last bite, he clapped his hands twice, and instantly, an older man wearing gray stepped in and gave the king a deep bow.

"Uncover the item I brought for the princess," he commanded.

The older man slowly made his way behind the king where a large item covered by a black cloth leaned against the wall. My heart rate increased as fear took hold. A gift from the king couldn't be good. The older man pulled it down. As the black cloth drifted to the floor, I squinted my eyes. King Madden didn't turn around, instead he stayed focused on me.

It was a large portrait of five people, a family. From where I sat, I could see an older man and woman sitting next to each other on thrones with crowns on their heads.

"The royal family," I muttered.

"Your family," he corrected. His gaze pierced through me. "I will reveal this portrait tomorrow night to help eliminate any doubt the people might have. But I wanted you to see it first to eradicate any uncertainty you might still harbor. Because you *are* the granddaughter of the late king and queen, and you *are* the lost princess." He finally broke our gaze and gestured with his head. "Take a closer look. If you don't believe it to be true, how will anyone else?"

I pushed my chair back slowly and made my way to the large portrait.

The man sitting on the throne must be King Davis. He caught my eye first. His dark hair matched his eyes, which gleamed with amusement somehow. It matched the small smirk pulling at his lips. He was handsome.

He was holding hands with a breathtakingly beautiful woman.

Queen Aleese was opposite to him in appearance—the light to his dark. I touched my hair, hanging over my shoulder. It was the same color as the queen's. And my bright blue eyes, which had always marked me as an outsider, were staring right at me.

King Madden's words came rushing back, "As *if your hair were not evidence enough, it's your eyes that give you away. You have her eyes.*"

BANG! BANG!

"Enter," King Madden answered.

I peered over my shoulder to discover an older guard standing in the doorway. His gaze fell on me, and for a moment, he seemed taken aback by my appearance. Whatever the look meant, it vanished as he looked back to the king and gave a small bow of his head.

"Your council is requesting your presence; they believe they have uncovered information about the reb..." His words died off as his gaze flicked back to me.

The king exhaled loudly. "Saying the council requests my presence would have been enough, Sal." King Madden tossed his napkin on the table and straightened his coat to leave. Prince Kasper followed. I wondered if they had forgotten my presence, but before King Madden crossed the threshold, his voice rang out, "Don't disappoint me, Little Fawn."

The moment he was out of sight, I returned my gaze to the portrait. I saw the truth, but it still felt impossible. I took in the rest of the painting and brushed the tears away on the back of my sleeve.

A young man, who looked younger than me, stood next to the king. He was an almost exact replica. However, his smile matched the queen's. Sitting between the king and queen, at their feet, was a little boy with a small wooden horse in his lap. He had lighter brown, curly hair and dark brown eyes that matched his father's. There was one more child, a young girl with the same blue eyes as the queen, but her hair was a darker blonde. She appeared to be somewhere between her brothers in age. There was something about her that pulled me in. And if I was to believe King Madden, one of the children was my birth parent.

I knew I was adopted, but I had never worried too much about my birth parents. I always thought they'd abandoned me, so why should I care about them? Plus, the parents who'd raised me loved me with all of their heart, and I was grateful to be theirs. But, if that was my family, they didn't abandon me. They were taken from me. Murdered.

Anger bloomed in my chest, and I couldn't stop the sobs. But it wasn't just anger. There was grief, and a desperate desire to know more about them.

"Ahem."

I jumped and found Prince Kasper standing in the room. His shoulders were tense and he looked extremely uncomfortable even though I was the one who had been crying my eyes out.

"I'm supposed to escort you to your room," he said, clenching his hands.

Feeling awkward and not wanting to leave yet, I turned my gaze back to the portrait. "Do you know which one was my father or mother?" I asked quietly.

"She was your mother."

Another tear rolled down my cheek, and I brushed it away.

"It's true then," I said, not expecting an answer.

"Yes."

"You believe it? You believe I'm their granddaughter?"

"Yes."

I tightened my arms around my waist while I stared at her face. I wished I knew her name.

But before I could ask, Prince Kasper said, "I need to take you back."

I turned to face him. "Why do you do everything he says?"

The muscles in his neck flexed, and his jaw tightened. "You can either come with me willingly, or I will carry you out of here."

I turned to memorize the faces of my lost family one more time, then I gave Prince Kasper a small nod, and we walked down the empty halls not saying anything. It wasn't until we turned the corner and saw the guard in front of my door that Kasper pulled me to a stop by grabbing my arm and then released me as quickly as he'd grabbed me.

"It's in your best interest to follow his orders." He rubbed the back of his neck. "You don't want to see what he's really capable of." He turned his back on me and disappeared.

CHAPTER 16

Raph

"WHAT HAPPENED?" ADIRA DEMANDED as Gil and I barged through the door carrying a barely-conscious Scat to my bed. He had been in and out the whole way back. The cloth I wrapped around his head bled through and left a bloody trail in our wake. Eitan took him from my arms and gently laid him on the bed.

"Oh my," Jules gasped as she peered around Eitan's back.

"I'll be back," Adira called before rushing out the door.

A soft moan drew our attention to the frail boy. His dark hair clung to his face with a mixture of sweat and blood. Eitan pressed a clean cloth against his injury.

"Who were those men? And why did they want him?" Gil asked as he brought over the water basin and more clean rags.

"I'm not sure," I answered sharply, incapable of delving into it.

Gil's eyes narrowed, but he dropped it, temporarily, knowing him.

I moved to the fireplace and leaned against its mantle. There was no room alongside the bed, nor anything else I could do. I took slow, steady breaths, hoping they would ease the tightness in my chest.

Bang.

The door hit the wall, and Adira rushed in with her arms full of supplies. "Make yourself useful," she ordered as she threw a bottle of alcohol at me.

Following her, I sanitized the needle she passed to me. None of us were healers per se, but Alon made sure we knew how to do a quick stitch job if needed. And Scat needed one. When I was done, I handed Eitan the bottle. Gil placed a piece of leather in between the boy's teeth before Eitan poured the alcohol on the wound. The leather instantly fell out when he screamed. Gil and Adira lunged to hold his thrashing body. They continued their hold as Eitan stitched.

I once again felt useless as I watched over the scene, so I paced near the fireplace. I had the poachers in my grasp, and now they were gone. I doubted their wagon would even be there anymore. I had no leads.

"Here." Gil handed me the bottle.

I took a drink and gave it back.

"Tell me what happened back there. Who were those men?" Gil asked. Eitan, Jules, and Adira walked over to join us. I peered over at Scat who was passed out with a bandage around his head.

"We call them poachers," I relayed. "They come to Llycia at least twice a year to capture street orphans and turn them into slaves. At least, that is what we assume."

"You can't be serious?" Jules wrinkled her nose. "Why hasn't the king stopped them?"

"Madden couldn't care less if a couple of dirty orphans no longer litter his streets," I spat out.

"Earlier, you said we..." Eitan trailed off, waiting for me to expound.

I pressed my back up against the cool wall and crossed my arms. "You already know I was..." I licked my lips while squeezing my eyes shut, but when I opened them and saw Scat, I swallowed the lump lodged in my throat. "I was, and still am, a Shade. I was actually the first one. Not the first street orphan, but the first one to bring us together. I created a life where we could survive easier and be somewhat safe."

"So you've encountered poachers before?" Gil asked, stealing a glance at Scat.

"Yes." I tried to block out her screams, which flooded my head. "My first encounter with them is what pushed me to start the Shades. Over the six years I lived on the streets, I saw dozens of kids be taken. Everyone tried their best to stay hidden, but hungry bellies drove kids to make reckless decisions."

"Man." Gil combed a hand through his hair.

"Does Alon know about this?" Adira asked.

"Yes. We have been trying to locate their place of operations for years, but every lead we get goes cold. Tonight, I had three of them right in front of me—"

"Raph, stop. You can't blame yourself for them getting away. If anything, it's my fault I didn't find you sooner. Those streets were too confusing. There's no logic to their design."

I shook my head, knowing well enough how labyrinth-like the streets were for outsiders.

"Do you think it's another kingdom?" Eitan asked.

"Could be." I shrugged.

Adira and Jules shared a look. "What did they look like?" Adira asked.

"There were two large men. One was your size," I said, nodding my head to Eitan. "I fought him off before a smaller one came and dragged Scat away."

"Did one of the larger men have a bald head full of markings?" Adira asked.

"Yes?" I answered.

"We saw them! They were leaving the palace early this morning," Jules blurted out.

"What?" I raised my eyebrow at Adira.

"We needed some fresh air and decided to get eyes on the palace. On our way, we almost got ran over by this wagon. We followed it to the palace where those three men dropped off some boxes and left."

"So Madden *is* in on it," Gil declared.

"It's not surprising." I rubbed my chin. "The question is what is he getting from it?"

No noise followed as we stared in different directions.

Eitan was the first to break the silence by asking, "What do we do now?" He tipped his head toward Scat.

"For starters, you can tell us wha' happened."

We dropped into defensive poses toward the open window where two people stood wet from the rain.

CHAPTER 17

Raph

TOMMY LEANED AGAINST THE edge of the windowsill with a large grin on his face, clearly pleased that he had snuck up on us. But he wasn't fooling me. I could see the worry etched into his brow and his quick glances toward Scat. Lemmy, meanwhile, was not trying to hide her concern.

"He's okay." I looked at her, but I was assuring them both.

"Poachers?" Tommy asked, his cocky grin gone.

At my confirmation, Tommy's hands clenched into fists. His face became hard, and he no longer looked like the carefree boy I had known. No. He carried the weight of the Shades on his shoulders. I knew exactly what he was feeling and the blame he was dumping on himself.

He took his eyes off Scat and met mine. "Thanks."

I wanted to tell him I didn't deserve his thanks, not until those poachers were stopped, but a noise from the bed pulled all of our attention.

"Tomm...Tommy is tha' you?" Scat's small voice called out. "Where am I?"

Lemmy ran over to his side, followed closely by Tommy. The rest of us kept our distance, giving them a moment.

"Man, kid. You jus' had to go and ge' yourself in trouble," Tommy joked while he assessed the bandage on Scat's head.

"Naw, I'll have a scar like you." Scat's voice was filled with admiration.

"Where'd you find him?" Tommy asked, taking a step away from the bed.

"Down by the docks, not too far from Stella's." I answered.

"Scat, were you followin' me and Lemmy?" Tommy turned his gaze to the little boy who looked like he was trying to sink deeper into the bed. "I told you to stay back and watch the others." He rubbed his hand down his face. For a moment, I was reminded of a similar scenario.

"Looks like you're getting a taste of your own medicine from the years that you ignored my orders," I said, then winked at Scat who smiled back.

"I wasn' tha' bad," Tommy argued with a small upward pull to his lips. "You jus' didn' know how to have fun back then."

"I've wondered what Raph was like as a kid," Gil stated, but he gave a leading look to Tommy.

"Oh ho, I can tell you countless stories abou' Raphy. Startin' with the time he stole a Farmer's prized hog from the Hub. Rode it all the way down to the docks." Laughter erupted around me. But no good memory of my time in Llycia came without the bad ones, so over the years, I'd learned to shut them all out.

"He did not?" Gil demanded, looking at me with a gleam in his eye.

"Sure did. Got many more like tha' one."

"Tommy, tell da one about the lady and...and...her shoe. Where he got her to believe he was some famous shoemaker," Scat blurted out from the bed.

"That's enough," I interrupted. "Scat needs to rest. Let's grab some food downstairs and leave him alone."

"Sure thing...Raphy." Gil gave me a mischievous look.

"I'll stay with him," Lemmy muttered to Tommy.

"Ge' me if you need anythin'." He gave Scat a last once-over before turning toward me. "Ran into one of Stella's men. Said this was for you." He removed a bag from his shoulder as he continued to walk toward me. "Along with a warnin' to keep your promise?" His eyebrow raised as he threw the bag at me.

Pulling the contents out, I recognized two servant garments and two white and black uniforms.

I threw a uniform to Gil. "Your dream of attending a ball is coming true."

He held it up. "It's not what I imagined myself wearing to a ball, but it will do."

"This is for you as well." I said throwing another item at him.

"Eww, what is that?" Gil dropped it on the floor, then picked the hairy item up.

"We can't have you drawing too much attention," I explained as Gil put a brown wig halfway on his head.

"How do I look?" Gil turned around, which caused the wig to fall over his eyes.

"Thanks, Tommy," I said.

"Don' thank me ye'. This is the easy par'," he said, eyeing the uniforms. "The fun comes tomorrow."

"You don't need to do this." I offered.

"Don' you try to take this from me. It's abou' time us Shades got a little payback."

Tommy's face was set. And if I was being honest, we needed him. I still didn't like the idea of him putting himself in harm's way.

"Relax, old man." Gil slapped me on the back. "Judging by the way those two just snuck up on us, you have no reason to be worried." He draped an arm around

Tommy's shoulder, ushering him toward the door. "Tell me some more about the great tales of little Raphy..."

The others followed, trying to catch every word that came out of Tommy's mouth. I rolled my eyes and looked back at Lemmy who was talking to Scat in a hushed tone. "Don't hesitate to grab us. We'll be downstairs."

"Thank you for everything." She gave me the same reverential look she had given Tommy.

Unsure of how to respond, I took my leave. If she only knew how much of a coward I truly was.

CHAPTER 18

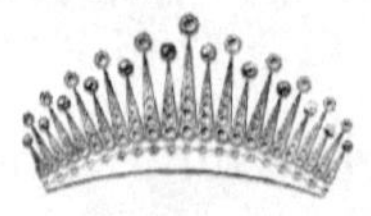

Talia

"JUST ONE FINAL PIECE and you're ready," Catherine said.

She and Malenee woke me before dawn to start preparations for the evening ball. I shuddered thinking how early they must wake people for events that occurred earlier in the day.

Her hands shook as she carefully walked toward me with a delicate gold circlet covered in small rubies. Malenee took it from her to place it upon my head. The muscles in my back tightened from the weight of it. It felt wrong. I felt like an imposter.

"Well?" I stretched my arms out with a shrug as they looked me over.

"You look like a queen." Catherine's eyes were glossy as she squeezed her hands together close to her heart.

"You're ready," Malenee added with a nod, then she lead me to the mirror on the vanity.

I wouldn't be able to hide from anyone at the ball. The dress was crimson, the king's color, and it screamed loudly of who I belonged to. The style of it was extravagant and showy. The neckline swooped and the lace edges brushed along my collarbones. There was more lace in the sleeves that acted like another layer of skin, going all the way to my wrists, covering my empty crest. The bodice was pulled so tight that I wouldn't be able to breathe all night. I also wasn't sure that I would be able to move with the heavy skirts flaring out from my hips.

I averted my eyes and took a deep breath. "Let's go over it again."

My nerves kept building. Anticipation and fear churned in my stomach like winds coming from different directions, fighting for dominance.

"Your Highness, it will all work out," Malenee said with kind eyes.

A firm knock came from the door. Malenee was first to take action. She didn't open it enough for me to see who was on the other side, but her response of a low bow let me know that there were two possibilities.

"Princess Talia," she had her back to me, "Prince Kasper is here to escort you to the ball."

My shoulders relaxed slightly. "Thank you, Malenee."

I strode over to the door as gracefully as I could, feeling the satin against my legs with each step. Malenee opened the door wider, and the Prince Kasper I had seen before was nowhere in sight. Instead, he wore all white with gold accents. His hair was slicked back, and a similar small golden circlet to the one I wore rested upon his head. The small amount of hair he usually had on his face was shaved, which showcased the length of his scar. A sword was strapped to his hip, and he truly looked like royalty.

He extended his arm, but I instinctively leaned away.

Malenee cleared her throat behind me. I placed my hand on top of his still offered arm, barely touching him. Then, without a word, he led me out of the room. He adjusted his pace to match mine as we walked down the hallway toward wherever the ball would be held in the labyrinth of the palace.

"Your appearance is befitting of a princess," he said, breaking our silence.

"That is the idea." I answered back, unsure of what his comment meant.

Nothing else was said as we continued on. My hands shook as the soft string music filled the halls. I knew he was aware of it as well, but he didn't say anything. He just stared forward. From the corner of my eye, I noticed that his white overcoat, which was tightly fitted to his large frame, had intricate designs stamped into the fabric in a crimson color, matching the same ones on my dress.

Prince Kasper slowed our pace as we approached two doors. He gave a nod to the guards, and they pushed them open for us. The music slammed into me along with many loud voices each trying to talk over the other. The air was filled with the smells of sweet liquor mixed with fruity perfumes.

We stepped through the doors and stood upon a balcony that overlooked a grand ballroom. Hundreds of people in fancy attire filled the room. Some were dancing while others stood along the sides having merry conversations with others. I got lost for a moment, watching the vibrant colors swirl together, and I forgot I was still holding onto the prince's arm. I lifted my hand off his arm slightly, and I noticed his gaze scouring the many people as if he was searching for someone. Everyone down there was oblivious to our presence except for one man.

In the front of the room, there was a raised platform where King Madden lounged on a golden throne with a chalice in his hand, staring right at us. He raised his chalice, and the music stopped. All eyes turned to him as he stood from his throne.

"Lovely people of Landore, I promised you all a grand announcement, and it's finally time to put your curiosity at ease." He walked over to a large piece of red fabric that was draped over something. He ripped it off, revealing the same portrait he had shown me last night. "Tonight, our kingdom shall celebrate! For I have found something that was long thought to be lost."

Gasps filled the room and people started instantly murmuring to each other. But they were silenced when King Madden raised his chalice again.

"When I heard news there was a possibility that a granddaughter of the late king was still alive, I sent my best guards to search for her. I was overcome with relief when I found her. Ladies and gentlemen, I present, Princess Talia, the lost princess of Landore."

King Madden extended his free hand in my direction, and every eye turned to look at me. In that moment, I truly felt like a little fawn in front of a group of hunters. The people below recovered from their shock and whispered to one another as they whipped their heads back and forth from the portrait to me.

I stared too and realized my hair was styled exactly like the late queen, my grandmother. We looked almost identical. It was deliberate.

Prince Kasper pulled me to the left where there was a staircase leading to the people below. I resisted his pull, unwilling to face those staring eyes and whispered comments up close.

"We have to go down," he muttered into my ear, giving a slight tug on my arm. Relenting, I leaned on him for support as we descended. I needed to; my whole body had gone numb.

Once we reached the bottom, the whispers ceased. It was as if time had stopped and everyone was frozen in place. The only sound came from the sharp click of my heeled slippers against the marble floor.

Prince Kasper led me through the crowd, which parted for us as we moved, most gave us a small bow or curtsy. But their stares didn't fall upon Prince Kasper, they stayed trained on me. I peered past the faces, trying not to look anyone directly in the eye. Massive candelabras circled around the border of the room, giving enough light to see but also providing a dark atmosphere that hung over the room. There was another circle of them encasing the balcony.

My eyes continued up to the domed ceiling that reached into the sky and reflected the starry night with small twinkling lights above. It took me a while to realize it was made of glass, and I was staring up at the actual sky.

My focus jerked back down as Kasper brought me to a stop in front of King Madden. His face was lit with excitement, but up close, I could tell it wasn't genuine. It didn't reach his cold black eyes. We bowed and King Madden walked down the platform to meet us. He placed a hand on Prince Kasper's shoulder and then turned to kiss the top of my hand. The same fermented smell of spiced liquor lingered as he pulled away.

"People of Landore, tonight we celebrate. Drink, be merry, and let us honor the return of Princess Talia," King Madden shouted.

Everyone cheered. A few went back to their dancing or conversations, but many gawked at me as if I was a ghost.

King Madden stepped closer to me. "Do not disappoint me tonight. I would hate to make an unnecessary trip to a small village." He didn't wait for my response, instead he gave a pointed look to Prince Kasper and ascended to his throne. Prince Kasper offered me his hand, and I raised my eyebrow.

"We are supposed to start the first dance," he whispered in between his teeth.

My eyes widened. I'd already forgotten everything Lady Celeste had taught me about what was expected.

Placing my hand in his, I allowed him to lead me into the crowd. The music transformed into a slow waltz as we reached the middle of the dance floor. It was one Celeste had tried to teach me, but I wasn't confident in the steps. However, Prince Kasper didn't give me time to hesitate as he led me through them. He was more rigid than Raph, my last dance partner. My thoughts went to that night, remembering the feel of his strong hand around my waist.

"You're sighing. Are you not enjoying the evening so far?" Prince Kasper's voice was low, and I started at the break in our silence.

"I wouldn't use that word to describe this evening," I stated flatly. Prince Kasper might not have threatened my life like his father, but he was no better.

"How do you feel?" he asked while he twirled me deeper into the dancing couples.

"Are you serious?" I hissed through clenched teeth. "You're asking me how I feel about your father threatening my parents if I make one mistake tonight?" My voice became higher as I tightened my grip. "Even if I do succeed tonight, he will forever hold those I love over me." I stared at him in disbelief. He tensed at my words like a knife had pierced his heart.

"It might not have to be that way," he replied.

"What does that mean?"

"My fath...the king loves to have control over people. But if you were to show him how loyal you are, without him having to threaten you, then he would reconsider—"

"Killing them?"

Prince Kasper's eyes showed almost a hint of caring, but I doubted it was over me and my problems. "Is that what you do?" My voice was thick with accusation.

His muscles tightened, but he refused to say any-thing. He turned his gaze from me, so I did the same, not caring enough to pry.

I looked around and noticed that there were differ-ences in the people. Some wore extremely expensive attire while others wore nice dresses and suits but of a lesser quality. One such lady wearing a bright green dress attracted my eye. There was something about her that was familiar. When I circled back to where she had been, her eyes were already locked on me. They were furious and appalled. The music stopped.

I broke her stare to bow to Prince Kasper, but he had already retreated, so I made my way to the outer edge of the room. But when I peered over my shoulder, my mouth went dry as I watched the lady in green come straight for me.

CHAPTER 19

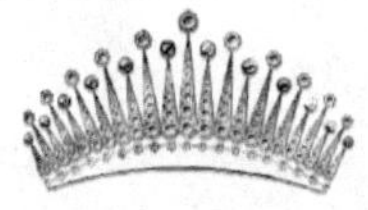

Raph

MY HAND CLENCHED AROUND the neck of another flute of champagne when I saw her standing on the balcony. My body tensed. I couldn't believe it was her. But I knew those icy blue eyes anywhere, however they weren't dancing with excitement like a little kid anymore. No. Her childlike joy had been replaced with something else.

Why was she holding the prince's arm?

Glass shattered under my grip, eliciting a squeal from the older lady I was supposed to be passing it to. Before she could create more of a scene, the room went eerily silent as Madden stood to speak.

"Lovely people of Landore..." he started his speech, and I eased through the crowd aiming for one of the dark alcoves while keeping Talia in my line of sight.

Tossing the broken glass in a pot, I stationed myself behind a pillar. "...Ladies and gentlemen, I present, Princess Talia, the lost princess of Landore."

My head snapped to Madden who was pointing at Talia.

My breath seized. Whispers filled the room, but all I could think was, not her.

For the last seven years, I had lived in Aydencia, and all I heard about was the lost princess. I always thought it was just a symbol for people to hold on to hope. I never thought she was real nor that she was Talia.

Alon knew the whole time. My chest rose as I clenched my fists. I was going to have some strong words for him when we got back.

An elbow jabbed my side, right before Gil muttered under his breath, "Is it true?" His eyes moved back and forth from the portrait to Talia, finally his eyes stopped and doubled in size. "He knew, didn't he?" he fumed, spinning to face me.

"It seems so." We watched as Talia made her way through the crowd toward Madden.

"What are we going to do? This changes everything," Gil lamented, itching his wig. A couple glanced over at us curiously.

"People of Landore, tonight we celebrate. Drink, be merry, and let us honor the return of Princess Talia," Madden shouted.

"We need to get back to serving," I mumbled, lifting my tray of drinks higher and doing my best to ignore the exasperated look Gil was sending my way. "I'll think of something," I added before turning away to offer drinks, which people greedily accepted as the whispers around the room grew louder, and the music picked back up.

I loaded my tray with more flutes as I tried to reform our plan to now incorporate getting Talia out too. Escaping was the part of the plan that already worried me the most.

Getting in had been surprisingly easy. Tommy's contact, who worked in the kitchens, notified us of some deliveries that would be coming in before the ball. All we had to do was knock out a few drivers and hijack their wagons before it reached the palace. The guards didn't look twice as we entered through the gates. We went our separate ways after that. Gil and I were disguised as two waiters, and our job was to keep eyes on the king and uncover what his big announcement was. Meanwhile, Eitan and Jules were in the kitchens getting as much information from the servants regarding any goings-on in the palace and where to locate any possible women held captive. At least Eitan and Jules would have already heard the news about Talia being the lost princess.

I righted my tray after some young lordling with over-ly greased back hair slammed his empty glass onto my tray.

I was also worried about Tommy and Adira since they were somewhere in the palace setting up a surprise for Madden. It would work, but there were risks.

Sticking to the outer edge, I easily spotted Talia across the sea of nobles because they gave her and the prince a wide berth as they made their way through the room.

This was going to make things harder. Talia being here, with every eye on her, changed things drastically. Plus, there was no way I could get word to Adira and Tommy about the change. Gil and I were on our own.

CHAPTER 20

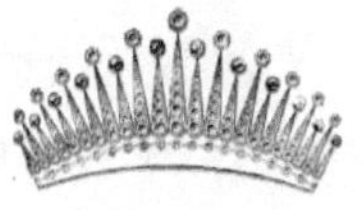

Jules

THE KNIFE SLIPPED THROUGH my sweaty hand for the third time. My gaze found Eitan who was standing across from me chopping onions at an incredible speed. He gave me an encouraging nod. I took a deep breath and pulled at my high collar, then I wiped my hands on my apron and grabbed the knife again. With slow movements, I finished chopping my first potato.

"I overheard Sophie telling Lily that she heard from Gideon that King Madden is going to announce the prince's future wife tonight," a young woman gushed to the woman beside me, as they decorated a cake.

"Well, that's not what I heard," a different one said as she rolled out dough on the counter.

The first two turned their heads at the same time.

"Out with it," one of them said, placing her hands on her hips.

"I heard it wasn't a wife for the prince, but for the king."

The two women broke out in laughter. "Don't be ridiculous."

"Stop this nonsense. Get back to work," the head cook yelled over his shoulder, quieting their giggles.

Since we had walked into the kitchens, the whole place had been abuzz with possibilities for King Madden's announcement. Everyone was so consumed by it that no one batted an eye when Eitan and I picked up a knife and started chopping vegetables.

"Good work," the head cook said, looking over Eitan's shoulder. "Come with me."

My eyes grew wide. Eitan placed his hand out, coaxing me to stay calm. He gestured to the pile of potatoes in front of me with his head before following the cook.

I continued chopping, but I didn't lose sight of Eitan. The cook had brought him over to the line of stoves. He was giving Eitan some sort instructions. Eitan nodded his head once and then turned to an open stove as the cook walked away.

I finished three potatoes before Eitan moved from the oven. He walked over to a pantry where a shorter maid was reaching for something on a higher shelf. His arm reached over her head and grabbed the bottle she had been trying to get. A squeal left her lips as she turned around and bumped into the shelves. I couldn't hear what they were saying, but after a while, the maid's cheeks darkened, matching her vibrant red hair. She covered her mouth as she giggled, then taking the bottle from Eitan, she scurried away.

He watched her leave before his eyes found me. I tilted my head with a raised eyebrow, but he shook his head at me and rubbed the back of his neck. I didn't fail to notice him looking over his shoulder, one more time, in the direction she had gone before he focused on whatever he was cooking.

"Shh. It's time."

The whole room went silent. Only the sound of food sizzling and the hum of the ovens could be heard. I inhaled, about to ask the woman next to me what was happening when a server ran through the kitchen doors.

"It's the...the..." He panted and placed his hands on his knees, "heir of the late king."

The whole room came alive, everyone was talking over each other. A deep V formed between my eyebrows. Eitan had dropped the spoon he had been holding on the floor. Someone whistled loudly, which brought silence to the room again.

"The granddaughter of the late king and queen has been found! The lost princess." The same server announced.

"Who is she?"

"What's her name?"

"I don't know, just that her name is Princess Talia," the same server answered.

It couldn't be. The potato I was holding slipped from my fingers.

"What does she look like?"

The server had to cup his hands over his mouth because the noise had picked up again. "She looks exactly like the former queen, blonde hair and everything."

My eyes snapped to Eitan, who was already focused on me. He nodded to the door. Keeping my head down, I made for the exit, and as I waited for Eitan to join me I paced.

"Do you think it's poss—"

"Shh." Eitan raised his hand, cutting me off as he walked through the door. Placing a tray of food in my hands, he gestured for me to follow him. We walked down the hallway in silence, passing other servers.

"How do you know where you're going?" I asked after the third turn.

"I don't, but I do know where the girls are being held."

"Where? And how?"

"The dungeon. It's going to be on the lowest level of the palace. The maid I helped mentioned it."

"She casually mentioned where young women might be locked up?" I looked at him.

He shrugged. "I have my ways."

"Gil better watch out," I said, giving Eitan a playful shove with my shoulder. "Wait." I stopped. "What about Tals?"

"Raph and Gil will get her," he said before stopping in front of me. "Trust me. They will do everything they can to get her out, but we need to focus on the young women."

Two maids turned down the hall, giving us both wide-eyed expressions as they approached.

"Excuse me ladies, we got hired for the ball tonight and have gotten lost," Eitan said with a playful smile. "They asked us to bring these down to the guards on watch in the dungeon. Could you point us in the right direction?"

They couldn't take their eyes off Eitan. One of them took a small step behind the other as she looked Eitan up and down.

"It's down that hall," the maid in front pointed. "Second door on the right."

"Thank you." Eitan dipped his head and both maids gulped in response before scurrying away.

"That is one way to get information out of people."

"Yeah." Eitan's shoulders depressed slightly as we found the hallway she had pointed to.

"It's because they don't know you."

The corners of his lips pulled down as he reached for the handle of the door. It opened to a set of stairs, which he started on before I could say anything else.

We descended using the light from the torches along the wall to guide us. A shiver went down my spine because the temperature seemed to drop. At the bottom, Eitan opened the first door he could find. It was a storage closet.

"We'll stay here until Adira and Tommy give the sign."

He followed me into the closet, closing the door partially.

"You shouldn't let people's initial reaction to your size upset you," I whispered to his back. He stood in front of me, keeping his face close to the crack. "I get it though. In Gasmere, people see me one way too."

He peered over his shoulder. "What do you do?"

"Pretend I'm oblivious to it. Sometimes I use it in my favor," I answered with a lift in my voice.

He let out a small chuckle before turning back to the crack. "I'm not used to it I guess."

"What do you mean?"

He quickly put his hand over my face as he leaned closer to the door. I leaned forward, straining to hear something, but I couldn't. Eitan reached for his hidden dagger, and I did the same with the one he had given me.

CHAPTER 21

Talia

"You are full of surprises," Elder Agatha spat as she stalked toward me. Her sharp face was pulled down by her scowl, but it was her familiar brown eyes that rooted me to my spot. They were the same eyes as those of her son and my childhood bully, Jacob Martin. Heat traveled up my neck at the memory of the last time I saw her as she stood in my house degrading Mother before the guards came. It felt like a lifetime ago.

I searched the crowds, half hoping her face would be among the countless others. But if Elder Agatha was here, then the elder with her would be her guard dog, Elder Derek.

"What lies did you tell in order to get the king to believe that *you* were the lost princess?"

I pressed my lips together to stop myself from snapping back.

"I was brought to the palace to answer for my crimes. When King Madden laid eyes on me, he declared me to be the granddaughter of the late king. I didn't trick my way into anything."

"You are nobody. Always have been. Always will be," she spat back. "You are not some princess—"

"Excuse me, Your Royal Highness." A young man, with a sharp nose, stood inches from me. I frowned and took a slight step back.

"May I have this dance?" He bowed with a flourish, and extended his hand to me. I was ready to deny him, but a movement from the corner of my eye reminded me of Elder Agatha's presence. I accepted the offer, and he led me through the middle of the other couples. The music was lively, and he lost no time in leading me into the dance.

"It's an honor to be your second dance of the evening, Your Highness," the young man said with an air of cockiness to him. "I'm sure with every other dance being already claimed, this will be the only chance I have with you."

I gave him a tight smile and leaned away. Annoyance passed over his calculating brown eyes.

"Excuse me for forgetting to introduce myself. I was so overcome by your presence that I completely forgot my manners. Lord Chaster at your service," he said with a small bow of his head. We step hopped around each other. "But you may call me Chas." His brown hair that was tightly pulled back into a low ponytail bounced with each step.

I opened my mouth to give him a greeting, but he spoke before I could.

"I'm the son of the duke of Trenton." His eyes met mine, waiting for me to respond. I couldn't have cared less who he or his father were, but because of the diligent work Celeste had done, I knew exactly who they were. His father was one of the king's closest advisers, which made me want to get as far away from him as I could. My eyes darted to the sides, hoping for some sort of escape, but instead they landed on the king who was staring right at me.

"It was a pleasure to meet you, Lord Chaster." My voice sounded strange, soft and frail.

The dance ended, but before I could catch my breath, another young man stole Lord Chaster's spot. I spent the next four songs dancing with random gentlemen. I couldn't remember their names. The more they talked about themselves and their titles, the more I drowned them out.

In my boredom, I scanned the different faces on the dance floor. They appeared joyous and merry, but when

I looked closer, I could have sworn I saw a layer of fear behind their eyes.

With one partner, I watched the servers and found them more interesting.

Straining my neck, I looked back because I could have sworn I knew that sharp jawline and those piercing green eyes, but they vanished into the crowd.

"Is everything okay, Your Highness?" my dance partner inquired, Lord Basthal, or Bazal, or something.

"Um…Yes, excuse me. I find myself suddenly thirsty."

Briskly, I walked to the outer edges of the room hoping to find some safety near the shadows. Finding some shelter next to a column furthest away from the king, I went back to scanning the servant's faces. I knew who I saw couldn't be him. It was best to believe it was a mistake. Still, the hole in my chest felt as though it burned a little larger.

Raph

I scanned the room, handing out drinks to the guests and searching for glimpses of Talia's pale blonde hair or a swish of her deep red dress as she was spun by yet another partner. Each new one made the knot in my stomach tighten.

Talia leaned back as far as she could, trapped in the arms of some bug-eyed lordling who was leaning closer to her. I dropped my tray on a table and nudged my way through the crowd, but two hands wrapped around my arms and yanked me to a halt.

"Raph, stop!" Gil's stern voice spoke in my ear. "You'll ruin everything. If you make a scene, we won't be able to get her out."

I slumped under Gil's grip, the fight draining from me. He released me, and we retreated to the outskirts of the room by blending in and doing exactly what two waiters should do. I didn't know how much more I could take when yet another pretentious son of a lord asked for a dance. I was about to find Gil and tell him I needed to cool off in the kitchens when a blur of red caught my eye.

Talia was leaving the dance floor and heading straight in my direction. I backed up into the shadows of one of the columns. She got close enough that I could see her flushed face and her chest rising and falling rapidly. She was stunning. But it didn't feel right. She didn't look like the Talia I had known. The real Talia. At least, the Talia I thought was real.

Standing so close, I could see that she was basically skin and bones. My free hand clenched into a fist as an overwhelming feeling rushed through me. It demanded that I wrap her in my arms and storm through the doors behind us. I inched closer.

Before I realized it, I was standing right behind her. I opened my mouth not knowing what I was doing when a voice called out to her.

Talia

"Your Highness," Celeste's overly sweet voice called out to me.

I causally tried to rub my sweaty hands on my skirts as she glided toward me followed by a group of young women with similar dresses and hairstyles to Celeste. I hadn't seen nor spoken to Celeste since she had confessed that she had hoped to be queen one day.

"Princess Talia." She bowed, and like a rehearsed dance, the five other ladies bowed in unison behind her.

"Lady Celeste," I acknowledged her with what I hoped was a true smile.

"King Madden requested that I introduce you to your other ladies-in-waiting now that you aren't preoccupied dancing with every eligible lord." Her voice didn't change, but it was the shift of her eyes that told me she was annoyed with it.

"Of course."

"Lady Marie, daughter of Lord Hanover." At her words a tall, slender woman stepped forward and bowed.

"Lady Olivia, daughter of Lord Reginald." A tall but curvy woman with similar light brown hair to the first, bowed next.

"Lady Mindy, daughter of Lord Dervin." She was petite with a small nose that fit her round face.

"Lady Philipa, daughter of Lord Chamont." Her hair was lighter with a hint of red to it.

"And Lady Astrid." She was short and curvy, but she looked at me with a true smile that reached her eyes. "Daughter of Lord Fisher," Celeste threw in, then flicked her gaze upward.

"I look forward to getting to know each one of you," I said, surprised by how easily the lie left my lips because I planned to never see any of them again after the ball. I expected them to leave once the introductions were done, but instead, they formed a semi-circle around me. And within no time, they were whispering about the people that passed by us.

"Oh my, I can't believe he actually came." A gasp left Lady Olivia's lips. All their heads turned in the direction she was looking. I even caught myself being curious as to whom she was referring.

"If I were Count Frederick, I wouldn't show my face until at least next season," Lady Marie, no, Mindy added in.

"Next year! Lady Sylvi chose a footman over him," Lady Philipa blurted and they started giggling except

Celeste. She only let a faint smile cross her lips before her eyes snapped to me.

"Please forgive us, Your Highness. We forgot for a moment that this is your first time at court."

Their eyes shifted to me and pity covered each of their faces.

"Lady Celeste told us of your upbringing," petite Lady Mindy said quietly.

Lady Olivia, who was standing next to Mindy, shuddered. "To think you were left alone, abandoned in the forest where any predator could have killed you."

My cheeks flushed at not knowing Celeste knew that about me.

"And having to grow up an orphan, in one of those villages, never knowing who you truly are..." Lady Philipa stated with the similar fake sweetness that Celeste used.

"I think it sounds fascinating." Lady Astrid gave me the same kind smile as before. I wanted to believe it was genuine, but so far, I didn't trust any of these ladies.

"Yes, if one were obsessed with commoners," Celeste muttered under her breath.

Astrid dropped her chin. I grabbed a handful of my skirts as I stared Celeste down. She returned my glare with one of her own.

"Ta...excuse me, Princess Talia," a male voice shouted.

"Who is that?" Disdain coated Celeste's every word.

Elder Cyrus's smiling face peeked through the crowd. My shoulders relaxed when a genuine smile crossed my lips for the first time that night as he made his way over to us. "This is incredible!" He gave a small bow. "I can't believe it. Wait until your parents hear word of this!" Elder Cyrus was the co-elder for the Healers with Mother, a close family friend. The sight of him made my eyes burn.

"It's good to see you, Elder Cyrus," I replied, my smile growing until I heard faint snickers from behind me. "I'm quite parched. Would you join me for a drink?"

"Of course, Your Royal," *hiccup*, "Highness." He bent over a little too far with his bow and spilled some of his drink on the floor.

"Excuse me, ladies." I grabbed Elder Cyrus's arm and led him to the drinks table. But I could still hear Celeste's voice ring out over the crowd of people.

"I can't believe King Madden allowed *them* to attend. It's embarrassing."

My grip tightened, which elicited a yelp from Elder Cyrus. "I'm sorry."

"It's all good, Talia. I'm so sorry, I mean, Princess. It's hard for me to wrap my head around it all," he said, scratching his head while he looked at me. "From the moment we found you in that forest, I knew there was something special about you. And look at you! A real-life princess." His words were hurried and a little slurred. Elder Cyrus had always been flamboyant and chatty, but there seemed to be no stopping him at that point. "To think, little Gasmere took in the lost princess. It's remarkable!" He raised his hands and more of his drink spilled. "We need to find Elder Agatha."

"Elder Cyrus," I placed my hand on his arm, "how is everything in Gasmere?"

He gave me a crooked smile. "Your parents are good, all things considered. They miss you and are extremely worried about what has become of you. This will surely cheer them up!"

I pressed my lips together. My heart broke imagining how much worry and pain I had caused them to bear these past months.

"Please tell them I love them, and that I'm sorry." If everything went according to plan they wouldn't be there when he got back to Gasmere but saying it out loud made me feel like they could somehow hear my words.

His face fell. "You have nothing to be sorry for. They are so proud of you, always have been. And when they find out you're a princess..." His smile grew again. "Although with the way the prince has been eyeing you all night, I don't think you are going to stay a princess for much longer." He wiggled his eyebrows at me. A shiver traveled down my spine at the feeling of being watched.

And there he was. Prince Kasper stood on the other side of the room staring at me. I took a step back, but he advanced.

"Princess, are you—" Elder Cyrus's words were cut off as the room shook and screams tore through the space.

CHAPTER 22

Jules

MY GRIP AROUND THE hilt of the dagger tightened when the sound of voices trickled into the closet. They were muffled and low, but they grew louder along with the sound of boots hitting the ground. It wasn't long before a shadow passed over the opening and the sound changed to stomping up the stairs.

Eitan's shoulders didn't relax until we could no longer hear anything other than our breaths. He had begun to turn around when a muffled boom caused the walls around us to shake. I lifted my hands over my head as items fell on me. The light around us darkened as the sound of metal clanging came from outside the closet.

"That's our cue. You ready?" Eitan whispered.

"Let's do this." Eitan pushed the door open and barreled out of the closet. I followed close behind, noticing some of the torches were littered on the floor.

We sprinted down the dim hallway.

Boom!

I placed my hand upon the wall to catch myself, then pushed off the moment I noticed Eitan hadn't slowed down.

"What's going on?" A voice shouted up ahead above the faint sound of cries.

Eitan slowed to a walk as we approached the end of the hallway. He peered around the corner and pressed himself against the wall, holding up two fingers to me. Holding his palm out, he disappeared out of sight.

I stuck my head out and saw a body already lying prone on the ground as Eitan held a guard in a headlock, his feet dangling off the floor. After a few seconds, Eitan lowered the unconscious guard to the ground.

Stepping out, I searched the area. A table sat in the corner with spilled drinks dripping onto the floor, and a few chairs were scattered around it. There was a ring of keys hanging from the wall nearest the table. The keys jingled when I took them down. Eitan stood under an archway leading to a hallway of doors, waiting for me. We followed soft cries to one specific locked door. I was tempted to open every door along the way, but who knew what King Madden kept in his dungeon.

I picked a key at random, but it wasn't until my fourth try that I heard the lock disengage. I looked to Eitan but he gestured for me to open the door as he took a step to the side hiding his large frame.

Huddled in the corner of the dark, stone cell sat a group of young women. Their dirty and hollow faces stared at me, streaked with tears.

I took a step into the cell. "We are here to rescue you."

At my words, another loud boom shook the room.

Raph

Screams ruptured my eardrums as another piece of ceiling crashed onto the floor. Shards of glass were everywhere. I pushed against the throngs of people and received an elbow to the eye as they trampled over each other desperate to get to safety. I scoured the crowd for her, but a sea of red flooded the room as the King's Guards made their way to Madden. I needed to find her. As I shoved a lord out of the way, I could feel the pressure around my heart.

A gap opened in front of me, and a flash of red crossed my line of sight. Talia stood wide eyed with an older man clutching onto her arm thirty feet away. She seemed uninjured, though there were a few tears in her dress. She wasn't focused on the chaos around her but instead she was looking across the room—to the prince.

He was pushing through the crazed mass, trying to get to her. She released herself from the man and retreated as if to make a run for it. She was frantically searching for a clear pathway until she saw me. Those icy blue eyes stared straight into me, and for a moment, everything ceased.

Another loud boom shook the room followed by more screams. A large candelabra crashed to the ground inches from where she stood, breaking our connection. Not wasting another moment, I ran toward her. She was twenty feet away when another candelabra fell in front of me. I had to roll to the side to dodge it, and by the time I recovered, she was gone.

I scanned the immediate area, and a frustrated groan ripped through my lips. The crowds of people were thinning, but she was nowhere in sight.

"Did you find her?" Gil yelled, making his way to me.

"She was right here," I answered, rubbing my hand through my hair.

"We'll come back."

"No."

"We have to go. If we stay any longer, we'll get caught. Raph, we'll come back for her."

Everything in me wanted to fight him, to say that we weren't leaving without her, but I knew the best course of action would be to regroup with the others.

I gave a curt nod. We sprinted to the nearest doors, throwing ourselves into the crowd, and getting lost among the people. I stayed sharp, searching for a sign of her.

CHAPTER 23

Talia

"Let me go," I demanded, ripping my arm out of Prince Kasper's grip.

He latched onto my other arm and continued dragging me down the narrow hallway, which was dimly lit and smelled of wet stone and stagnant air. I could only hear our footsteps echoing in the space.

I fought against his hold, chastising myself for hesitating. If I hadn't, I might have made it out to find Catherine and Malenee. But Elder Cyrus had grabbed onto me the moment the room shook. When I finally pried my arm from him, I could have sworn I saw Raph again, which was impossible.

But after the candelabra fell, Prince Kasper and I briefly made eye contact as I picked up my skirts to run in the opposite direction. I didn't get far before his viselike grip clamped down on me. The stupid dress, and its ridiculous layers of skirts had slowed me down. He pulled me through a door behind the dais King Madden had been sitting on.

The sound of clinking metal drew my attention to his hand as he pulled out a ring with keys on it. He stopped us in front of a wooden door. It took him no time to find the right key to open it and shove me inside. I barely caught myself until I grabbed onto a nearby table for support.

He walked past me, and without a glance or a single word, he rifled through a cart that was near two plush chairs. They weren't the only things in the small room. On the far side, pushed against the wall, were two small cots and next to those sat multiple pillars of crates stacked upon each other.

Prince Kasper turned and plopped into one of the chairs as he threw back whatever drink he had made. He sat with the empty glass, moving it back and forth while staring into it.

His arm cocked back and I jolted when the glass broke against the wall. Clutching my chest, I tried to calm my racing heart, but the fear wouldn't be tamed. He didn't come for me though, he sat there staring at the broken glass on the floor. I stood there, awkwardly keeping one hand on the table for support.

King Madden slammed the door open, stormed into the room, and cursed under his breath. The same older guard from the dinner came in behind him and locked the door.

"That was the end of my leniency," he fumed as he paced. "Those rebels will be no more. I will not rest until I have destroyed every last one of them, and anyone who associates with them." He turned to the guard. "Sal, I don't care what it takes. Blow up every mountain until you find their hideout. I want them all destroyed!"

Prince Kasper approached his father and handed him a glass, which he guzzled greedily, releasing an exhale after he swallowed. The mad fire in his eyes lessened slightly. Finally, he sat in one of the chairs and handed the glass back.

The table beneath me moved, but when I peered down, I noticed it was my trembling body that was moving, not the table. I tried to calm myself by wrapping my arms around my waist.

King Madden accepted a second glass from Prince Kasper. "Did they try to go after her?"

My arms squeezed tighter as Prince Kasper looked at me and hesitated.

He shook his head. "No, I got to her before anything could happen. The chaos they created must have been too much for them to handle."

Releasing my breath, the worry inside me lessened, but only briefly. What happened to Malenee and Catherine? Were they safe?

"I want a group sent up there right away. Double the watch posts," King Madden commanded to Sal.

"I can take a group tonight," Prince Kasper volunteered.

"No. You are needed here. Sal, send my best men."

"Yes, Your Majesty." Sal gave a bow of his head, but I didn't miss the way his triumphant eyes taunted the prince.

"Father, what if their base isn't in the Northern Mountains? We have been searching for years, and we haven't seen a trace of them."

"They're there," King Madden declared.

"Couldn't it be possible that they are hiding out on Karden? If you allow me a few men, I will go and report our findings," Prince Kasper offered.

My feet shuffled forward, interested in the western island off Landore. It was on a map in one of the history books, but besides it being a part of Landore, I knew nothing about it.

"Oww!" The table screeched across the floor and my toe throbbed. Three sets of eyes looked at me as if I had crashed their secret meeting.

"Little Fawn." The king's voice almost purred my nickname causing small bumps to cover my entire body. "By no means have you proven yourself, but you didn't do bad tonight." He rubbed his chin as his eyes continued to analyze me. "Yet my other surprise for the night was ruined."

"What surprise?" The words came out weaker than I hoped.

His signature predatory look emerged, but before he could answer, another guard entered the room.

"Your Majesty." He bowed to King Madden first. "Your Highness." He spoke with a bow to Prince Kasper. "Your Highness." He said the last one to me. My mouth parted slightly.

"Get on with it," King Madden grumbled with a wave of his hand.

"The palace is secure." The guard shifted his weight.

"Is that all?"

"We were unsuccessful in obtaining any rebels." Sweat dripped from his face.

"Why is everyone so incompetent!" He stalked toward the guard. "Anything else?"

His eyes flicked to Prince Kasper and then back to the king. "There was a problem in the dungeon."

"And what problem was that?"

Unintentionally, I stepped away, and my back pressed against the wall.

"It seems like their main objective wasn't to infiltrate the ball, but to get access to the dungeon."

Withdrawing his sword, King Madden held it to the guard's throat. "Spit it out."

"They freed the women."

A yell ripped through the room. I slammed my eyes shut, knowing exactly what would happen. I pressed myself further into the wall as the thud, that could only be a body, hit the floor.

CHAPTER 24

Raph

"SHE WAS RIGHT THERE!" Pain ricocheted up my arm as I punched the wall. A few screams broke out. "Adira, get them out of here." I threw my hands into my hair and continued pacing.

"You need to calm down," Gil said, eyeing the few young women who had already started to cry. "We will get her out."

"And the night was successful. We got them out." Eitan threw his head in the direction of the small pack of girls huddled next to the fire.

I stared at their faces, but all I could see was Talia. "I failed her."

"Stop it." Jules's fierce eyes landed on me as she walked away from the women. "We can spend all night throwing blame and reliving the past, but it isn't going to get us closer to saving Tals."

"She's right. Start from the beginning again, and try not to lose it this time," Adira said while passing out some bread.

"I'll start," Gil offered. "We were doing our jobs, serving the snobby elite. I was doing a bang-up job at it. I had already emptied my tray four times before—"

"Gil," Adira chastised.

"Okay. Madden greeted everyone and then, in a grand flourish, he unveiled this large portrait of the late royal family. It took me a while to believe it was them since the only picture we've seen of King Davis and Queen Aleese is an old faded one where you can hardly make out anything other than that they are sitting on thrones and wearing crowns. Which really, that could be any—"

"Gil!" we yelled at once.

"Alright. Everyone, relax," he said, holding his hands up. "He then shocked everyone by announcing how he found the lost heir of the late royal family. And who did he point to? You guessed it, our girl, Talia, who was standing on the balcony looking like the spitting image of the late queen. It was a little freaky if you ask me."

"No one is." I placed my hand on Gil's shoulder. "We knew that the plan would need to adapt. The only option was to wait and use the chaos to get her out. I trailed her the whole time until...I lost her."

"Was it because of that old lady?" Gil asked, amused. "She was all over you."

"Yes." I pinched the bridge of my nose. I'd failed to mention that I'd distanced myself more than I should have after I almost blew our cover. "Then the first explosion went off." I nailed Adira with a glare.

"It wasn't our fault. We weren't the only ones looking to create a distraction. We had to light them early," Adira explained, crossing her arms over her chest.

"What?" I asked.

"I tried to say something sooner, but you were throwing a tantrum." She matched my look with one of her own.

"What happened?" I lowered my voice.

"Tommy and I were making our way to the throne room when we overheard a guard and a couple maids talking about staging a fire."

"That's brilliant," Gil exclaimed. "Why didn't we think of that?"

Ignoring her brother, Adira continued, "We had to move up the timeline."

"You did the right thing. But that is interesting..."

"Do you think it was Gale?" Eitan asked.

"Could have been. But there's no way to know for sure. And Alon was adamant that we not try to contact him," I said.

"What happened after the first explosion?" Jules asked, standing next to the young women who were all intensely looking at me.

"I found her shortly after. She was with an older man, but she was focused on the prince who was fighting his way to her. It seemed as though she was about to make a run for it, until…" I raised my hand to rub the back of my neck. "Until she spotted me. She froze and then the second one went off. A candelabra nearly landed on her. I was twenty feet away when the third one went off and almost got taken out. By the time I recovered, she was gone."

"That's it?" Jules's eyes were wide. "You lost her and don't know if she escaped or if she was taken by the prince? What if she is out on the streets, right now! All by herself."

"She didn't escape," I stated.

"How do you know that?" she countered.

"Because guards were posted at every exit. Gil and I had to swap clothes with a few noblemen to get out," I answered.

"I'm definitely keeping this jacket," Gil said, pulling at the lapels. I had already discarded mine once we got out of the palace.

"So now what?" I could hear the defeat in Jules's voice.

"We do what we always do." Eitan gave her a sympathetic smile. "We make a plan."

"Starting with returning them back to their villages," I said, throwing my head to the five women who were red-eyed and covered in dirt. "Jules and Eitan, will you go get them some food and ask for some rooms to accommodate them? We can't do anything tonight. They need rest."

"I want to be involved in the plan," Jules said.

"When you both come back, we will start planning,"

Satisfied with my answer, she gently helped the women exit my room. Eitan followed after the last woman.

"This isn't going to be as easy," Adira said.

"I know."

"He is going to have guards everywhere now, especially on her."

"I know."

"And if she is the lost princess—"

"Adira, I know!"

CHAPTER 25

Talia

Late Spring

HE HAS ONLY SAID two sentences since I arrived two months ago. "Your Royal Highness" was how he greeted me when we first met, with a dip of his head. But nothing else. His dark brown eyes looked through me as if I wasn't even there.

Two weeks later, at one of the engagement dinners, he asked if I wanted another drink. He called over a waiter and then left me without another word. This has been the extent of our communication. And today I'm supposed to marry him!

I wish he was a jerk or at least conceited. I could handle that. That is what I was expecting, not for him to ignore me every time we were around each other. Everything he does drives me insane! From his wavy, brown hair which *rests above his eyes to the way they light up with mischief when he talks with his friends. It's infuriating. How in the world are we to be husband and wife? He doesn't care for me, none of them do. I'm unwanted and alone.*

I had spent most of my time these past two days in bed reading the journal, never letting it out of my sight. The despair that had been living inside of me continued to burn stronger since the ball, but it grounded me in some way. I still hadn't learned the name of the princess who wrote it. I hadn't learned much at all, other than that she had very few interactions with her future husband. But something about her writing resonated with me. I was reading an entry written on the day of her wedding when I was summoned by King Madden.

My footsteps fell like lead, and my eyes stayed focused on the red in front of me as I followed a guard to the king. I could feel the journal pressed against my waist underneath my skirts. It gave me some sense of strength, since I had no more hope.

A part of me wondered why he requested my presence since I'd been locked in my room without a word for the past two days—no visits to the library, no training with Celeste, nothing. The only people I had seen were Catherine and Malenee, but we didn't talk much besides them explaining to me how the explosions weren't their doing. They believe someone besides the

Northern Rebels had planned something the night of the ball and it interfered with their plans.

"Your Highness." The guard was holding the door open, waiting for me to enter.

Something was different in the throne room. It was still bare and void of life, but there was something else.

"Little Fawn," King Madden rejoiced. Perched on his throne, he held a stack of papers in one hand. His seemingly happy mood made me trip over myself. Luckily I caught myself before I could fall. I continued the long walk to the dais, and his eyes gleamed with excitement. Prince Kasper stood in front of the throne with his arms behind his back.

"I have splendid news to share with you both."

I stopped to the right of Prince Kasper. Had he found the rebels and captured them? My mind spun, thinking about what good news to him would be. But then I saw it.

A crack in the wall behind his throne.

Squinting, I noticed not just one but many cracks running up the wall and onto the ceiling. Looking at them brought me a small sliver of joy.

"We are going to proceed with our plan." He waved the papers, which seemed to resemble letters.

"Plan?" I asked, knowing good and well that the prince wasn't going to say anything.

"These letters will be sent out to announce your engagement."

I went still. Part of me thought or hoped that with everything that had happened, the wedding might be off. I should've known better.

"In turn, the esteemed members of my court will host parties in your honor to celebrate the engagement. You will *both* go to them together. A united symbol of our families and of your love."

I cringed at his last word. The journal on my hip burned hot, reminding me of the princess's situation. I chanced a glance at Prince Kasper. He was as stoic as ever, but there was a slight shake to his shoulders.

"This will lead up to your wedding in a month's time."

"A month!" I couldn't hold back the horror I felt.

"Father, won't more time be needed to get everything arranged?" Prince Kasper broke his vow of silence.

"I'm the king! If I want you two married tomorrow, it would happen." His eyes turned to slits as he leaned forward. "Do you both understand?"

We dropped our heads in unison.

A few knocks came from the closest door. "Come in," King Madden called out and Sal, the older guard, walked in.

"Have you located it?" The king's face changed into something I hadn't seen before. It was close to desperation.

"No, Your Majesty." Sal dropped into a deep bow. "I have twenty guards scouring the palace as we speak. We will find it."

"You better hope so, Sal. Because if you fail me..."

"Understood, Your Majesty," he said, backing out.

"Wait." The king brought up his hand. "Escort the princess to her room."

"I can escort her." I jumped from Prince Kasper's voice of urgency.

"I love to see you falling in line, my son. But no. There is more I need to discuss with you." He waved Sal over with his hand.

The prince's hands tightened into fists as Sal stalked toward me. His face was round and hard, his eyes hungry, and he favored his right foot. Everything inside of me recoiled and yelled for me to run away. Forcing myself to keep a somewhat normal pace, I headed for the door before he had the chance to lay a hand on me.

Even in the hall, I kept a couple paces ahead of him. I was fairly confident that I could find my way back to my room. It was on that side of the palace, two floors up. Thankfully, with every turn I made, there was someone occupying the hall. We passed a group of men who were part of the King's Court talking about a hunt before we turned onto an empty hall. My body went cold.

"One would think you were afraid of me, Your Highness." Sal's voice was low and made the hairs on my neck stand up. "I would hate for that to be the case." His stride quickened until he was in front of me. Not wanting him to touch me, I backed away, but there was a wall behind me. His eyes lit up.

The air around me grew thin. I yearned, with every-thing in me, for someone to pass by. But he continued to leisurely step closer. It was when I could feel his hot, foul breath against my face that something in me snapped.

I placed my two hands against his chest and pushed as hard as I could. "Step away." He stumbled back, shock written all over his face. "You will never talk to your future queen like that again. Actually, I never want you to utter a single word to me again."

Without giving him an opportunity to say or do any-thing, I picked up my skirts and ran the remaining distance, not stopping until I slammed the door shut behind me. I grabbed my chest desperately trying to calm my erratic heart.

"Your Highness," Catherine's voice squealed. "Are you okay?"

Not able to form words yet, I gave a nod. She and Malenee made their way to me, worry etched on their faces.

"I'm fine," I breathed out. And I was. Whatever hap-pened back there made me feel strong and powerful.

"What did the king want?" Catherine asked.

That feeling vanished. I was nothing but a puppet. Pushing off the door, I made my way over to the fire. "Just to remind me of my job as his little pet."

CHAPTER 26

Jules

"WE NEED TO BE doing something. I won't sit here doing nothing for one more day." I pressed my hands on the table and pushed the chair out from under me.

"I get it," Gil said, using his hand to direct me to sit back down. His voice was husky and low. I had woken him before dawn and dragged him downstairs so we could catch Raph before he left.

"Then why haven't we left this place for three days?" I flopped back down in the chair. "And why won't he tell us where he goes every morning?"

"I don't know. You're right though. We need to hit the streets."

"You need to talk to him." I moved my gaze to the stairs.

"I will," he said, rubbing his face.

"Why are you so apprehensive about it?"

"It's complicated."

"I'm sure it's not," I said and crossed my arms.

He let out a deep chuckle. "You're so stubborn."

I flashed him my teeth before pressing my lips together and raising my eyebrows.

He exhaled. "Raph has history here."

"So?"

"The type that leaves scars."

I dropped my gaze as I bit the inside of my cheek.

"In the past, the more I'd push him about what happened, the more he froze me out."

"I understand," I said, keeping my eyes down. My throat burned as I fought the wave of emotions.

"Hey. It will get better." Gil's golden eyes were usually filled with mischief but they burned into me with a strong intensity that made me look away again.

I swallowed a lump. "We still need to be doing more for Tals."

A creaking sound had us both looking to the stairs. Raph peered at the door directly behind us before turning his gaze to us.

"Come grab a seat." Gil said as he pushed a chair out with his foot.

Not removing his gaze from Gil, Raph sat. Silence followed as they both waited for the other to speak first. Raph's lips pressed into a fine line.

"We don't have time for this." They both released their stares as I slammed my hands on the table. "It has been three days since Adira and Eitan left with the women, and we haven't done anything. We don't even have an inkling of a plan to rescue her." I clenched my fists, glaring at Raph.

"I'm working on it," Raph muttered.

"That's the problem. You leave before the sun comes up and don't come back till it sets. You refuse to tell us where you go or what you're doing." I softened my voice, "I know you have personal battles you're facing, but this isn't about just you."

"You're not the only one who failed Talia that night," Gil said, his stare focused on the table.

"If we want to save her, we need to do this together. You need to let us in," I said.

"You're right."

I opened my mouth ready to deliver another argument before I snapped it shut. "Wait, what?"

"I should have included you two." Raph rubbed the back of his neck.

"Yes, you should have." I nodded my head, but my eyes were still wide.

"Where have you been going?" Gil asked.

"Nowhere really."

"Raph." Gil leaned forward, placing both hands flat on the table. "Don't freeze me out. I know you're hurting. We are too."

"Okay," Raph said, locking eyes with Gil.

A moment passed between them before the left side of Gil's mouth lifted. "What's the plan then, boss?"

"We hit the streets," Raph said, then gave Gil a knowing smirk. "We need to find out what Madden's plans are with Talia. I want you two to go out and see what you can find."

"What will you be doing?" I asked.

"I'm going to reach out to Tommy and see what he knows."

"Wait. You haven't reached out to him yet?" My chin dropped. "What in Landore have you been doing this whole time?"

The veins in Raph's neck protruded as his face turned ashen. I was about to retract my words.

"It doesn't matter," Gil's voice cut through. "We need to focus on res—" A patron walked through the door. "On our jobs."

"I expect a detailed report from you tonight," I said, pointing my finger at Raph's chest.

He dipped his head in my direction.

"Alright then." Gil clapped his hands together. "Let's get out of here."

CHAPTER 27

Raph

LLYCIA WAS WAKING UP, or for some, going to bed. The streets were hazy with the morning fog, but I could make out people stumbling their way back to wherever they were staying. The creaky sound of wooden wheels hitting the stone echoed through the streets as the Merchants headed for the Hub.

I, however, walked in the opposite direction toward King's Court, the district where all of those who consider themselves nobility shopped and lived. By the time I reached their clean streets, the fog had dissipated, and the sun was breaking through.

"Watch where you're walking," a well-dressed man barked at a Farmer, showing the canyon between the villagers and those deemed "worthy" of being a part of the King's Court. But it never stopped the visiting villagers from coming and gawking at how the rich lived.

I brushed against the storefronts, hoping to overhear something.

"Wonderin' when you'd show up again." Tommy stepped up beside me. "Didn' think it would take three days."

"I've been busy."

"Yeah. The docks can be a busy place, especially in winter." Tommy gave me a sidelong look, fishing for information. He continued when I didn't give him anything, "You won' find a lead. They know how to cover their tracks."

I clenched my jaw and stopped at a fancy dress shop. "Have you heard anything since?"

"Crickets."

I nodded. Something would get out eventually. We just needed to be the first to know it.

The sound of pounding feet against the stone street had us both in a ready stance. Coming directly toward us was a horde of young women. They weren't running yet, but their brisk pace told me I didn't want to get in their way.

Tommy and I backed against the shop wall as two of them fought for the lead. They didn't slow down until they came to the same shop we were next to. They formed a long line outside the door and waited for the owner to open. A woman with dark, shiny hair and red lips stood at the front with a triumphant smile on her face. But the further down the line, the more distraught the faces grew. I looked at Tommy, but he had the same bewildered expression I did.

"I hope she doesn't run out before it's my turn," a young woman with curls said.

"I will die if I have to wear one of my old dresses," a taller one replied.

"I wouldn't go," the one with curls replied.

The other one's eyes grew to twice their size. "I wouldn't miss these parties for anything."

"I still can't believe someone would marry him." Her curls bounced as she shuddered.

"I can. He is dark and mysterious."

"But he has...you know..." The girl with curls tilted her head and sliced her finger along her neck.

"So? It means he could protect me from any threat," the taller one said with a far-off look in her eyes.

"Shh," the woman standing in front snapped.

The first two women pressed their lips together trying not to laugh.

"She's just upset because she doesn't have a chance at becoming queen anymore," the taller one whispered.

My fists seemed to clench on their own when the girl with curls couldn't hold back her laughter anymore.

Tommy gave me a questioning look, but I shook my head.

"Look! She is opening the door," someone in the crowd screamed, which elicited a bunch of high-pitched squeals.

They filtered into the shop. When the last one went in, Tommy was the first to speak, "Guess tha' answered some questions."

"Yeah," I said, pushing off the wall.

"Who is she?"

"What?"

"The princess who is marryin' the prince," he explained as he matched my strides.

Pressing my tongue on the roof of my mouth, I took a breath. "She is a friend of ours. She is being kept against her will."

"The one you were after?"

"Yeah."

"And now she gettin' married?"

"No," I barked, before catching myself. "We will get to her before then."

"Have a plan?"

My back muscles pulled tight, not wanting to answer. Our pace slowed because we were getting close to the district's borders where the houses were less grand.

"You better find out about these parties. Sneakin' back into the palace would be a death sentence."

"I know." I stopped and raised my head to the sky. "I wish we had someone on the inside that could communicate with her."

"What about a letter?"

"Huh?"

"My guy could deliver a letter to her."

"That could work." I was already formulating a plan.

"Only one. Can' risk more than tha'."

I gave him a nod. "One is all I need."

CHAPTER 28

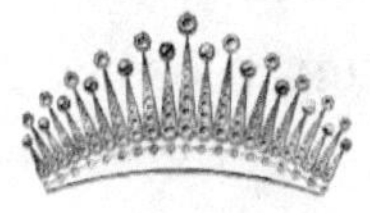

Talia

A GUARD OPENED THE door for me, and I entered the room with a new stack of books. Everything was back to how it was before the ball besides the guard that never left my side, and I could barely find the motivation to get out of bed. I had even given up on the journal, not finding anything of value so far. The only thing that helped was the king's library where I tried to find anything I could on the late king and queen, my family.

"While you were gone, this letter was slipped under your door," Malenee said, coming to stand to the side of me. She extended a small folded piece of parchment.

I stared at it, then slowly reached to take it from her hand. "You don't know who sent it?"

"No."

"It's mysterious," Catherine said, leaning around Malenee.

I looked at the piece of paper. All it said was one word, but it was enough to warm my chest.

Caffrey.

I trembled as I stared at my name. The lines were hard and short as if written in haste. It wasn't familiar, but then again, I had only ever seen my parents' handwriting and King Madden's—I knew instantly it wasn't from him. No. There were only two people in all of Landore who called me Caffrey.

Taking my time, I unfolded the piece of paper. My eyes jumped to the bottom, but there was no signature. It was blank. Unable to contain my curiosity, my eyes devoured the written words.

We know your current situation. If you want out, we are here to help. Outside of your prison, we are waiting in the shadows, watching. Find a secluded spot, and we will meet you there. You're not alone.

I flipped the paper over in denial that there wasn't more written. The words were cryptic. I knew who had written them. I could hear his low, raspy voice as I read it. My heart pounded against my chest as I read it over and over again.

"Your Highness, are you okay?"

Forgetting my surroundings, I gazed up to see Catherine and Malenee staring at me with pinched brows and tight lips. I looked back down at the piece of paper, envisioning Raph sitting down to write it. I brought my hand to my mouth and tried to stop the smile from forming.

"Yes. I'm more than okay," I said with a small chuckle.

They turned to each other with deeper Vs between their brows. I extended the letter out for them to read. Catherine reached for it first as Malenee stared at me.

"I don't understand," Catherine said, handing the letter to Malenee.

"Do you know who this is?" Malenee asked while rereading it.

"I do."

"Who is it, and what does it mean...Your Highness?" Catherine said, shifting her weight from her toes to her heels.

"It means that there is still hope." I didn't try to hide the smile that spread across my face. "My seven strangers haven't forgotten me."

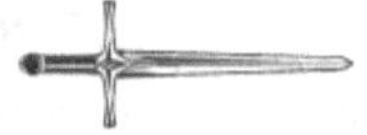

I was curled up in front of the fire unable to tear my eyes away from the journal when the sound of the doors opening startled me.

"She's gone," Catherine cried out, staring at my still made bed.

"Your Highness," Malenee found me by the fire, "have you slept?"

I peered over my shoulder at the windows and saw light breaking through the curtains.

"No, but that hardly matters," I said, jumping from the chair in my nightgown. "I found it! I finally found it." The excitement was too much for me to contain. I felt alive for the first time in weeks. Everything inside me trusted that I would be rescued. Because if anyone would be able to save me from the king, it would be them. The hope had created a fervor inside me to try and do my part even though I was confined behind the palace walls. And what I discovered from the journal would change everything.

"Found what, Your Highness?" Catherine asked with a smile.

"The truth! It's awful, horrific. But it's what we need to end him!"

"Please, Your Highness, slow down. Start from the beginning." Malenee offered me to sit again. I refused, instead pacing the floor in front of them.

"This journal belonged to Queen Aleese, wife of King Davis, and my grandmother." I stopped for a moment to look at their faces, which were a mix of disbelief and shock. "And she knew who murdered them!"

"Wait, what?" Malenee asked, blinking rapidly.

"Here, let me read it:

"*Where does the time go? It feels like yesterday that I was an unwanted prisoner behind these walls, but now, all of my greatest memories live here. Stephen will be fourteen tomorrow and will start his combat training. In a blink, he went from being little George's age to a young man. And Adeline isn't far behind him. She is basically a young lady who won't stop growing. All of her dresses are too short. There are moments where everything seems perfect, but they don't last long. There is something dark lurking in these halls. Like the cold winter air sneaking through a crack in the walls. It's putting me on alert for when the next attempt will come.*

"*I have tried to talk to Davis about it, but he has always had a blind spot when it comes to him. His loyalty and unquestionable love for his family prevents him from seeing the truth. But I see it.*

"*From the first day I came to this place, I saw it. There was a deep hatred in Charis's heart that passed to her son, and it has grown deeper and stronger throughout the years. It's no coincidence that the first attempt on Davis's life happened the day Stephen was born. I need to do something. For each night, I awake from my sleep with the same dream. Charis standing over our dead bodies soaked with our blood while he stands next to her with a bloodied sword.*

"I'm afraid he is lost. Not even Davis, his only family, can reach him. I fear Madden will do anything to fulfill his mother's wishes."

A stillness came over the room when I stopped talking, and a chill went through my body as if I, like Queen Aleese, could feel the cold air at my back.

"This—"

"This is exactly what we needed," I said over Malenee. "If we were to get this to whoever was in charge of the rebels it would change everything. It would show the people of Landore what really happened to the late royal family. Another kingdom didn't kill them. It was him." My eyes flicked to the door as I finished.

"Oh," Catherine's eyes grew wide.

"Excuse me, Your Highness, but I don't know if that is enough," Malenee said with a quiet voice. "Just because...she thought King Madden carried ill feelings toward the late king doesn't mean he murdered the royal family."

"But you know what he's capable of."

"Yes, and I'm not saying I don't believe what the late queen is implying." Malenee stepped closer. "But I think we need more proof."

"I haven't finished it. There's still more ent—"

The door opened, and I hid the journal behind my back.

"I'm sorry, Princess Talia," Celeste said with a bow. "I was worried." Her eyes rested on my hidden hands before she moved to look at my attire. "We've been waiting for you in the ladies' parlor, but I see you're not ready," she finished with a glare in Malenee and Catherine's direction.

"Yes. I was feeling unwell. But I'm better now. I'll be there shortly."

"Glad to hear it, Your Highness," Celeste said, turning to leave.

"Lady Celeste."

"Yes, Your Highness."

"Do not enter my room without being invited in."

"Of course, Your Highness. My apologies." She bowed and shut the door.

I exhaled releasing the book. "I swear she came hoping to catch me doing something wrong."

"It seems that way." Catherine shook her head.

"We should get you ready, Your Highness," Malenee added.

"Yes. I can't leave them waiting for too long. Who knows what rumors Celeste has already started."

CHAPTER 29

Talia

THE LADIES' PARLOR WAS exactly what it sounded like: a room full of women. Men were never allowed in, even servants. It was where women of the King's Court spent their time, but who knew what they actually did. Today was my first day visiting the room. Now that everyone knew that I existed, King Madden wanted me to spend as much time as possible with the other ladies of the court.

"Her Highness, Princess Talia," the guard announced from the other side of the door as I walked through with Malenee and Catherine behind me. Everyone in the room bowed and then froze, staring at me. There were about twenty women in all.

"Welcome, Your Highness," Mistress Pennier said, walking toward me. "We are glad to hear you're feeling better."

My eyes instantly found Celeste who was standing in the middle of the same group of women that I met at the ball. A slight sneer flitted across her face before it changed to her trained smile.

"Yes, as am I."

"Come, everyone is very excited to have you here." Mistress Pennier led me to where a group of women stood in front of chairs that formed a circle. The room was twice the size of the room I stayed in. It had similar large windows that opened up onto a little balcony, and the walls had the same pattern, but instead of lilac they were cream. It was bright and very different from the other rooms I had seen in the palace.

We approached the women, and they all held the same taut fabric on circular frames, similar to what Celeste would work on when I would read.

"Please take a seat, Your Highness." Mistress Pennier said, pointing to an open chair next to Celeste.

I peered behind me, but Catherine and Malenee had retreated to the edges of the room next to some other maids. The moment I sat, everyone else followed and resumed their work and conversations.

I looked around the room at the other women. Some were standing near the window talking in hushed whispers, stealing glances at me. There was another group at a table on the far side playing some sort of game. Everyone in the room was fairly young except for Mistress Pennier.

"Your Highness," a woman sitting a few chairs down from Celeste spoke up. I had met her at the ball. It was either Olivia or Marie. "Are you looking forward to tomorrow's hunt?"

"I'm not sure." Silence filled the room as everyone looked at me. "I've never been to a hunt." Everyone released their breath at the same time.

"Oh, it's a wonderful time. You'll love it," Marie (I finally remembered) said.

"What do we do if only the men are allowed to hunt?"

"We wait," Celeste commented.

"Until they come back." Marie's knees bounced with anticipation.

"I see." I tried to hide the boredom in my voice but failed.

"There will be games and food for us," Astrid said with her genuine smile. She was sitting three chairs from my left.

Celeste whispered something to Philipa, which caused her to snicker.

"That sounds like the best part to me," I said to Astrid, feeling Celeste's eyes on me.

"What about Prince Kasper winning the hunt?" Philipa asked, appalled. The sunlight made her hair look even redder than it had at the ball.

"What about that?"

A chorus of gasps filled the room.

"I'm afraid Princess Talia is not aware of this specific tradition," Mistress Pennier said, placing her needlework in her lap. "It's from an old tradition. When a man and a woman get engaged, a hunt is organized. In order for the man to be deemed worthy of marrying the woman, he must be the one to successfully hunt the stag."

Instinctively, I prayed with all my might that Prince Kasper would fail, and I wouldn't have to marry him.

"If Prince Kasper doesn't get the stag…"

"Oh, don't you worry, Your Highness," Mistress Pennier threw her hands out in front of her. "The tradition isn't taken literally anymore. Plus, Prince Kasper is the best hunter in Landore, after the king that is. You have nothing to worry about."

My posture dropped slightly. I tried to cover it up with a light smile and nod of my head.

The conversations picked back up. Mistress Pennier gave me a piece of fabric and a threaded needle, but I had no idea what to do with it. It sat untouched on my lap as I gazed out the window, wishing I could be back in the room reading Queen Aleese's journal.

"Oops," Celeste said as her fabric dropped next to my feet. "I know you're up to something," she whispered while reaching for it. "I'm going to figure it out."

She straightened and continued her work. The back of my neck felt like it was on fire. Had she seen the journal in my hands? Did she somehow know that Raph had gotten a message to me? No, she couldn't have. But I felt a warning go off. I needed to be careful around her.

CHAPTER 30

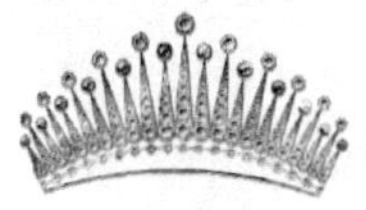

Talia

THEY WERE NOT LYING when they said we waited. The men involved in the hunt left before the sun rose, but we didn't arrive at Lord Vic's estate until midmorning. I didn't understand the point of us being there at all. For the ladies entertained themselves with the same activities they did in the ladies' parlor.

"Would you care for anything to eat, Your Highness?" Astrid asked with a semi-clumsy bow.

"No, I'm fine." I answered, sipping on the same drink I started with. I'd positioned myself on the edge of the room closest to the tables where the ladies were playing games. I hoped that people would assume I was trying to learn the game and leave me alone. I needed to figure out a way to get out of the room so Raph would have an opportunity to rescue me.

"Are you enjoying yourself?" she asked.

"Yes," I answered, focusing on controlling my tone.

"Truthfully, I despise these parties. I would rather be out there," she said, casting her gaze toward the windows, "or reading."

"Now that is something I can agree with."

We shared a small smile.

"Princess Talia, I hope you aren't getting too weary standing over here," Celeste's melodious voice had an extra bite to it as she floated in our direction, the other four of my ladies-in-waiting directly behind her.

"Not at all. I was enjoying myself."

She didn't respond, but her glare said plenty.

"Would you care to play, Your Highness?" Philipa asked, extending her hand in the direction of an empty table.

"That's a wonderful idea." Celeste's eyes turned calculating.

"No, thank you. I'm good with watching for now."

"Learning Landore's traditional game is a part of your training, Your Highness. The king will expect it." Celeste knew exactly what she was doing and gave me a triumphant smirk.

Anger took over as I led the way to the empty table. Placing my drink down, I took a seat, and they followed.

"Let's play Tutten," Celeste directed while the other girls gave each other knowing glances.

"I don't think that's the best idea. Anyway, we don't have any coins," Astrid said with a broken voice.

"We will do what we always do. We will gamble with secrets," Celeste said, picking up five dice and rolling them onto the table.

The game consisted of rolling dice and trying to guess if you would roll higher or lower than the person before you. There was no real strategy involved. Mother, Father, and I loved to play games at night, but the games we played always dealt with some strategy. A sharp pain went straight through my heart at the thought. I still hadn't heard word that the rebel contact had gotten them out safely.

"Ooooo," the women broke out in a chorus as Olivia guessed wrong.

"What is the real reason you didn't go to Lord Chaster's party?" Mindy asked, since she had rolled right before her.

"I..." Olivia dropped her chin. "I couldn't find a dress that fit."

A fit of giggles broke out as Olivia kept her head down. Astrid gave me a small shrug and shook her head. I took a fistful of my skirts and tightened my grip.

"Lower," Marie said as she picked up the dice and shook.

With a clammy hand, I grabbed the dice. "Lower," I said and threw them down. My throat swelled as I counted the dice. Everyone looked at Marie.

"Your Highness, are you looking forward to marrying Prince Kasper?" she asked.

Everyone's eyes bounced to me, their mouths opened. Wiping my hands on my skirts, I opened my mouth and said the truth, "I'm nervous." I leaned back slightly as they melted in their chairs a little, everyone except Celeste. Her eyes continued to pierce through me.

"Being married one day terrifies me," Mindy said, leaning forward.

"Not me. I can't wait to be the lady of the house." Philipa threw her hair behind her.

That opened the door for them all to share their feelings about one day having to marry someone.

"I believe it's your turn, Lady Astrid," Celeste said, raising her voice over everyone else's.

Everyone closed their mouths and Astrid, with a slow hand, picked up the dice. An audible exhale left her when the count came out lower.

Celeste was next. "Higher." My breath seized as the dice fell from her hands. She threw a threatening look to Astrid who was trying to keep a calm expression. I knew exactly what question I would ask. It was one that had been pressing on my mind since before the ball.

"What...I mean who—"

"They're back!" Someone yelled from the window.

"Aww, too bad," Celeste said standing from the table. The other women had already done a clumsy bow as they rushed to the windows.

"Next time." I placed my hand on Astrid's shoulder as I stood and found my way to a corner. No one paid any attention to me. I glanced at the door closest to me. It could be my chance. With quiet steps, I made my way over to it. I checked behind me when I reached for the handle. No one was looking. I turned it and pushed against the door. I flew forward as it was ripped from my hands. I caught myself by grabbing onto the frame.

"Going somewhere, Your Highness?" a guard asked, staring down at me.

"No. I was just...just wanting some fresh air."

"We can open a window for you if you'd like?"

I waved my hand in front of my face. "No need. I'm okay now."

The sound of male voices echoed from the hall. Behind me, I could hear the women rush around getting into position.

"Yes, Your Highness."

Stepping back into the room, I pressed myself against the wall furthest from the doors. I pressed my lips together and watched the men walk into the room. My opportunity was gone. Prince Kasper was one of the last to walk through the door, but the moment he did, everyone stopped what they were doing and bowed.

No one would look him in the eye. He searched until he found me. His eyes darkened slightly before he turned toward the refreshments. I released a breath, but my relief was short lived as I saw Celeste and the others make their way toward me.

"Your Highness." They bowed as they took their stations around me. As my ladies-in-waiting, they were required to constantly be by my side, which was another problem I had to solve.

Not wasting any time, their whispers flittered back and forth, gossiping about the lords and ladies in the room. I tuned them out in favor of staring out the window wondering where Raph and the others were. Could they be outside waiting for me?

"Excuse us, ladies." Prince Kasper's voice made me jump.

He was standing right in front of me. My ladies-in-waiting bowed, then scurried away from us. He offered me a drink, and I took it without a word. We stood there, in silence, which was better than the whispers filling my ears, but it had me feeling on edge.

"How was the hunt?" I asked.

"Successful."

Inwardly, I deflated at his response.

"How was it here?" he asked.

"Awful."

His shoulders moved from a single laugh. "I can imagine. If it makes you feel better, it wasn't much better out there." He threw his head toward a circle of lords. They resembled a group of girls gossiping.

"What? You mean you don't enjoy discussing the latest court scandal?"

"Never."

I finally turned to look at him. "You don't give off that impression." Silence followed. "Who do you hang out with during events like these?"

"No one."

I bit my lip debating whether I should ask or not.

"What about Lady Celeste?"

"Don't let her get to you. She's like her father."

I lifted an eyebrow.

"Lord Daven has been climbing his way into my father's inner circle for years. He would do anything to gain a higher status, even auction off his only daughter."

"So were you two betrothed?"

"Only in their minds. My father would gain nothing from that arrangement."

I gazed out among the people until I found Celeste. Her eyes were already fixed in our direction with a scowl.

"Like I said, don't let her get to you, but don't let your guard down around her either." He was staring at me, and for the first time, I didn't feel terror course through my body.

"Can I ask one more question?"

"You may."

"Who is Lliana?"

The moment her name left my lips, I was filled with regret. Whatever civility had been between us was instantly ripped away. His eyes went back to being dark and distant, his muscles tightened, and he refused to look anywhere but straight in front of him.

"I'm sorry. I was curious."

The silence between us felt suffocating. I bowed and took my leave, but I heard his voice behind me. "She's a reminder to never let yourself care for anyone."

I turned, but he was already walking away. A strange feeling latched onto my heart, but I pushed it down deep. The prince wouldn't be my problem for much longer.

CHAPTER 31

Talia

Subconsciously, I pushed the needle in and out of the taut piece of cream fabric, not following any sort of pattern. My focus was far from what my hands were doing and from the conversations that were happening in the ladies' parlor. Queen Aleese's journal was what invaded my every thought. I finished it a week prior, but there was no more mention of King Madden nor his mother. Instead, the majority of the entries talked about her children, my mother, Adeline, and my uncles. I devoured every word, wanting to know everything I possibly could about them.

A loud snort pulled me from my thoughts as Mindy covered her mouth while Olivia whispered in her ear.

I couldn't help but imagine my mother spending her time in the room with Queen Aleese and her ladies, trying to act like a young lady herself. I stopped moving the needle. Something inside of me reached out for more. I yearned for the room to show me what they were like when they lived in the palace.

"Princess Talia?" Shaking my head, I noticed Mistress Pennier standing in front of me with a furrowed brow.

"Yes?"

"I said we need to go over the ceremony, Your Highness."

"Right." I tried to swallow, but the moisture had left my mouth. The wedding was a week away. I did everything I could not to dwell on it, but it was getting more and more difficult since wedding preparations took up the majority of my day.

"As you know, a royal marriage ceremony is handled differently than a regular one," she said, reminding me of the main differences. There were a ton of extra traditions and rituals that didn't make any sense. Her voice went in and out as I thought about Raph and the others.

It had been almost three weeks since I received his letter, and I hadn't seen a single sign of them. I also hadn't been able to isolate myself. Three parties had been thrown in honor of the Prince and me. At each one, I was either consistently followed by my ladies-in-waiting or Kasper was by my side. Rubbing my hands on my skirts, I tried not to fret about how tomorrow night's party was the last one before the wedding.

"Before the vows, you and Prince Kasper will show your eternal connection by drinking from the Blood Chalice."

"What!"

"No need to worry. Drinking actual blood stopped many years ago. You and the prince will be drinking wine out of the same chalice." I leaned back against the chair. "After that, a cord will be tied around your waists, and you will forever be bound as husband and wife."

Cringing at her words, I noticed many of the girls had come closer to hear Mistress Pennier. Most of them had excitement in their eyes, but a few looked apprehensive.

"Do you know what your dress looks like, Your Highness?" Marie asked, having stopped her needlework to listen.

"Uh, no. I don't."

"I'm sure it's going to be breathtaking," Astrid said from the other side of me.

"Yes, no doubt." Marie said, sharing a smile with Astrid.

If anything good had come from the past three weeks, it was that the other women were finally accepting Astrid.

"Of course, it will be," Celeste's haughty voice cut through. "You will look good in anything, Your Highness."

Everyone stared at Celeste with a look of shock. Over the past three weeks, she had become insufferable. All the other women had distanced themselves from her. Even Philipa no longer stayed around her.

"Thank you, Lady Celeste."

She gave a soft smile as she bowed her head. She was up to something.

"I can't believe it's a week away," Olivia gushed.

"I still haven't decided on what dress to wear," Mindy moaned, then placed her face in her hands.

One by one as they described their dresses, each one would look at me for my approval. It made me feel terrified down to my core because these women not only accepted me, but they respected me.

CHAPTER 32

Raph

"It's been three weeks, and we have nothing to show for it," Jules said, dropping her face into her hands. "We need to try something else."

"You're right," I said as I leaned against the mantle of the fireplace. Her head snapped up when Gil spit out the drink he had taken a swig of. And, of course, it went all over my bed. Closing my eyes, I forced a breath into my lungs. "It's time we take a more active approach."

"What do you have in mind?" Gil asked, wiping his mouth with the back of his sleeve.

"We know that there's another party being thrown tomorrow night, and it will be at some noble's estate."

"We've failed at finding a way in the past three times," Jules muttered.

"Yes, we can't break in. Madden has cracked down on securing each entry and exit with his guards. But what if we remove that obstacle?"

Gil's face scrunched up as he tried to piece it together. "I'm lost."

"Are you saying that we make it so we don't have to break in?" Jules asked, still not fully understanding.

"Yes. If we force the party to change from inside to outside, we won't have a problem with breaking in."

"That would give Tals a greater chance at finding an opportunity to sneak away."

"Hold on," Gil said, raising his hands. "How are we going to make a house unusable except for the gardens? What if they move the party to another estate?"

"It will have to happen about an hour before the party starts. We will need to find something that can only be found in the Kingdom of Nefali."

"You know that party is in less than a day," Jules said, rubbing her temples.

"Stella's!" Gil shouted.

"Who's Stella?" Jules asked, looking between the two of us.

"An old friend who has exactly what we need," I answered.

"This is our last chance. We can't fail. Are you sure this will work?" Jules furrowed her brows.

"Yes." It *has* to.

"What if she has given up hope?" Her voice croaked. "Or what if the first letter never reached her?"

"Should we send her another one?" Gil asked, placing his hand on Jules's shoulder.

"No. All we could risk was one." I said with a shake of my head.

"The wedding is a week away. Is the risk bigger than us potentially failing and her marrying the prince?" Jules argued.

I threw my head back with an exhale. "I'll talk to Tommy, but I can't promise anything."

She nodded her head, but her eyes were still clouded with worry.

"I'll meet you two at the docks within an hour."

"You sure you don't need some help writing the letter this time?" Gil asked as one side of his face pulled into a smirk. He had walked in on me when I was attempting to write the first one.

"An hour." I walked to the door and opened it for them.

"This has to work," Jules whispered, as she paused in front of the doorway.

"It will."

Shutting the door, I walked over to the small desk. I sat staring at the blank piece of paper longer than I could afford. With the first letter, I had to make sure I made it vague enough that if someone discovered it

Talia wouldn't be held responsible. It had taken me over fifty tries to get it right.

"Ahhh," I moaned, placing my head into my hands. I needed to stick to what was essential. I couldn't risk it reading like an escape plan.

My heart picked up speed the moment the thought entered my mind. It would work, but could I do it? Heat traveled up my neck as I thought about the words I would have to write. With a shaky hand, I forced myself to write the words as they formed in my mind a little too easily.

How can I survive another day in this constant torture? Knowing you feel the same, yet not being able to be with you. Every day I walk among the gardens, pretending you are there with me. I sit among the hedges, waiting for you to come find me. Do not waste another day, put me out of my misery. Come to the gardens. I'll be waiting.

Yours

CHAPTER 33

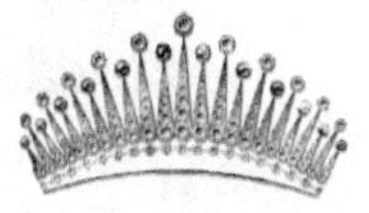

Talia

"YOUR HIGHNESS, TRY AND hold still," Malenee scolded with laughter in her voice. She was brushing some powder onto my eyelids while Catherine worked on my hair. But no matter what, I couldn't get my knees to stop bouncing.

Catherine's hands had stopped, so I looked at her through the mirror. She was staring at me with a single tear on her cheek.

"Is everything okay?"

"Of course, Your Highness," she answered, wiping the tear away and resuming her work.

But I knew it wasn't. They both had been acting strangely since I let them read Raph's letter. I could feel the color in my cheeks as heat traveled to them. At first, I had been in denial that the letter could have come from Raph, but the handwriting was unmistakably the same as the first letter. It wasn't until the fourth time I read it that I realized it was a hidden message disguised as a love letter. They hadn't given up on rescuing me, and at the last party they would be waiting for me in the gardens. All I had to do was figure out a way to ditch my ladies and Kasper. I swallowed down the lump in my throat. I could do it.

"All done, Your Highness," Malenee announced, stepping away from me.

I stood and allowed them to help put me in the dress made for tonight. It was by far my favorite dress that I'd had to wear. The silk was soft against my skin and the two-layered skirts were light and easy to move in. It was as if the dressmaker was aware of the escape plan because even the dark blue color of the dress would help hide me within the shadows.

"Perfect," Catherine said.

The lump in my throat came back as I turned to look at them.

"Please, reconsider."

Malenee put up her hand while shaking her head. "We aren't allowed to come. It would draw too much attention if we did."

I had tried to convince them to come with me, but they had adamantly refused.

"But—"

A firm knock resounded throughout the room. We stayed unmoving, staring at one another, knowing that it was our goodbye. Giving a small nod to Malenee, she walked to open the door. I followed, knowing it was Kasper to escort me like he had for the other parties.

"Your Majesty," Malenee said, dropping down into a deep bow.

My heart stopped as King Madden leisurely walked into the room. Giving a rushed and clumsy bow, I kept my eyes focused on the floor.

"Leave us," he ordered.

They scurried out of the room, but I briefly caught their sad and worried faces.

"You have made quite the impression on my court, Little Fawn." His tone was masked by his predatory stare. "You even had me convinced."

I furrowed my brow.

He advanced. "I thought I had given you enough examples to stay obedient. But, alas, it looks like I may need to break you further."

"Your Majesty, I have no idea what you're talking about. I have done nothing besides what you have asked."

"Lies," he yelled, circling behind me. "When did I tell you to take something of mine."

I spun around to see him holding up a book that looked identical to Queen Aleese's journal. My eyes flew to where I had stuffed it under my mattress and then back to the book he was holding.

"I...I..." Shaking my head, my throat constricted. "I found it. It was in the library. I had no idea it was yours."

"Lies!" He slapped the book against his hand. "How long have you been working with them? Did they reach out to you at the ball?" His nostrils flared as he waited for my answers.

"No. I'm not working with them."

"You may think you're irreplaceable or that you have some sort of hold over me by being 'the lost princess,'" he said, coming closer. "But let me tell you a little secret," he leaned forward so he was whispering in my ear, "I picked you to be the lost princess."

I took two steps away. An evil sneer formed on his lips.

"There is no lost princess. None of them survived!"

"But the portrait, and..." I reached up to touch my hair.

"Yes. You do share the physical traits of the Vasderians, which made this all much more believable. But many children showing other kingdom's physical traits have been abandoned, left to die. You were the lucky one that survived."

I opened my mouth and tried to form an argument about how he was wrong. That I was the lost princess. That Queen Aleese and King Davis were my grandparents. My fight died on my tongue instantly. He had said what I already knew deep down.

"If you breathe a word to anyone about what is inside of here," he waved the journal in front of my face, "you will see how cruel I can be."

He stepped back and looked me over. "Freshen up. You have an image to uphold."

Wiping the tears from my face, I watched as he left the room, leaving me defeated and crushed.

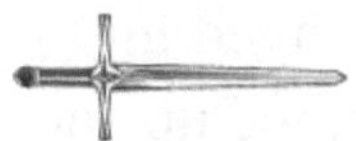

"Are you okay?" Kasper whispered as he led me down the illuminated path toward the back gardens. "You seem...different."

"I'm fine."

"Did something happen?"

"I said, I was fine." Pulling my hand from the crook of his arm, I quickened my pace. It was taking all of my strength not to fall apart. I hadn't been able to process what happened because Kasper showed up seconds after King Madden left. It felt like a huge hole in my heart had been gutted, one I hadn't known I had filled. I slowed my steps, knowing I couldn't enter the party without being on his arm.

He re-extended his arm to me but didn't say a word. We continued in that silence until the path opened, revealing the many guests.

The moment Kasper mentioned the party had to be moved to the outdoor gardens for some unknown reason, I felt a surge of confidence go through me. Raph and the others had done their part, but now it was my turn.

"His Royal Highness, Prince Kasper, and her Royal Highness, Princess Talia," the herald announced. Everyone bowed as we stepped into the party. I wanted to scream for them to stand up and stop bowing to me. It was all a lie.

Kasper led us over to where drinks were being served from a lady's skirt. She wore a dress that held the drinks on a metal contraption with holes for the stems of the glasses to be placed in. She grabbed two from her hip and offered them to Kasper and me. Wrapping my fur cloak tighter around me, I denied her offer, but Kasper took both.

Burying my emotions, I observed my surroundings, instantly spotting hedges on the other side from where we stood. That had to be where Raph would be waiting for me. A dance floor was marked by columns, and it was in between me and the hedges. No one had started dancing yet, but when they did, it would be a decent cover. But I needed to escape Kasper's watchful eye.

"Are you cold?" he asked, staring at my trembling hands.

"No, I'm fine." I placed my hands inside my cloak and tried to stop my body from shivering. I wasn't cold, but the pressure was getting to me. It was my last chance to escape.

"We should probably start the first dance." He extended his hand, and I accepted. We stepped onto the dance floor, and the musicians started to play. Not too soon after, everyone else joined in and for the rest of the night the dancing wouldn't cease. Marie and Olivia were the first two to join us with two young men. Shortly after, I could no longer see past the sea of dancing couples. It was time.

The moment the music came to an end, I slipped out of Kasper's hands, weaving in and out of the couples in a semi-crouched position. I was almost through when a loud crash came directly from my right.

The lady holding the drinks was on the floor with shattered glass surrounding her. A dark hooded figure was near her, but not for long because they were headed in my direction. I hesitated, wondering if it could be Raph, before I ran toward the hedges. I slipped on the wet ground, and by the time I recovered, I felt a firm grip around my cloak. I heard shouts in the distance, but I couldn't see anything as the hooded person dragged me away. I fought back and was surprised when I fell to the ground as their grip released me.

I pushed to my feet. Kasper stood next to me pointing his sword at the hooded person's throat. "Reveal yourself," he commanded.

The person pushed back their hood to reveal an older man covered in dirt. He stood tall and unflinching when Kasper's sword touched his neck.

"Who do you work for?"

The man's eyes flicked to me. He gave a small bow of his head before making a move for me and screaming, "LONG LIVE KING DAVIS!"

Kasper moved fast, and in one smooth arc, he sliced the man's head off.

I covered my mouth as the man's head fell away from his body. Screams broke out. Kasper stood over the man's body with blood dripping from his sword. His eyes were dark and empty. I stepped away.

At my movement, his eyes found me, softening for a brief moment before becoming hard again. "Are you hurt?" he asked while signaling some guards over.

I shook my head and wrapped my arms around my stomach.

He sheathed his sword and came closer. Specks of blood were scattered across his face. He offered his arm, but I pulled away.

"You should probably clean up," I said, noticing more blood on his jacket as we walked closer to the party.

"I can't leave you alone."

"I'm not alone." I tilted my head toward the crowd that was still fixated on us. "You can't go back to the party covered in blood."

"Fine, let me call some guards."

"No need. Lady Astrid!" I waved her over. She had been standing on the outskirts of the crowd.

"How will she protect you?" He turned back around and called out to two guards that were helping with the removal of the body. "They'll be watching your every move." He leveled me with a stare before he walked away. He knew what I had been trying to do.

"Your Highness," Astrid said in a breathy voice.

"Go get Lady Marie."

"Yes, Your Highness." She gave a quick bow and scurried away.

The two guards Kasper had signaled kept pace on either side of me, staying about two body widths away. I made my way back, knowing that my best opportunity of escape would come from the crowd.

I had finished a lap around the party before Astrid and Marie found me.

"How can we help, Your Highness?" Marie asked.

I took a step closer to Marie, trying to gauge her height to mine. "I'm needing a moment alone to collect myself after what happened, but those two guards won't leave my side. I was wondering if you two might help me?"

I could feel the sweat at the nape of my neck as they looked at each other before looking back at me.

"Of course, Your Highness." They said in unison.

CHAPTER 34

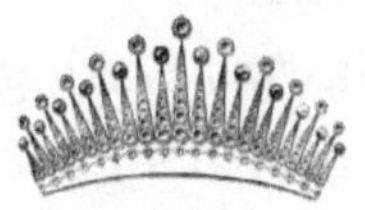

Raph

THE SOUND OF SHATTERED glass and screams forced me out of hiding. I had moved myself deeper in the small maze of hedges after a couple tried to have an intimate moment a little too close.

"Reveal yourself!" Prince Kasper stood in front of Talia with his sword pointed at a hooded figure. Instinctively, I reached for a dagger prepared to throw it if the prince were to fail. The figure pushed back his hood. He looked to be older, around Alon's age. I had never seen him before.

"LONG LIVE KING DAVIS!" he lunged for Talia, and it took everything in me not to do something, but the King's Wraith didn't hesitate. He sliced the man's head off.

Returning my dagger, I watched as he tried to comfort Talia, but her fear of him was evident. I clenched my fists and forced my legs to stay rooted to their spot. She was so close. I could be next to her within seconds.

The prince signaled to some guards as they walked back toward the party.

"Lady Astrid!" Talia was waving someone over. The prince called for two of his guards, then said something to Talia before he turned and left her. The young woman who she called over must have been one of her ladies-in-waiting. A few words were exchanged before the young woman scampered off. I moved a little closer to the edge, needing to follow Talia's every movement. She was up to something, and I needed to be ready when she made her move.

Eventually the same lady as before approached Talia, but she wasn't alone. Another young woman, who was much taller, stood next to her. Talia shared some words with them that made both of their backs straighten.

"Can you believe one of them got in?" A high-pitched voice to my left said, causing me to duck behind the hedge.

"It wouldn't have happened if she wasn't here," another voice said.

"It's a good thing Prince Kasper was close by or who knows what would have happened to Princess Talia."

"Yes, if it wasn't for the prince…" I didn't need to see her body language to know that whoever had spoken was not a fan of Talia.

"Can we go back to the party? It's creepy over here."

The first one didn't reply, but I could hear the footsteps grow distant. Lifting my head, I scanned the edge of the dance floor. Talia and her two ladies were no longer in the same spot.

A commotion drew my eye to the far side. A circle had formed with everyone looking down to the ground. It wasn't until a gap opened that I saw two guards standing in the middle holding someone up. It was one of the ladies with Talia.

I moved my focus and saw a glimpse of Talia's cloak that she'd been wearing, but she wasn't moving. She was fixed to that spot with her hood up.

Come on.

I moved further into the shadows. Footsteps were nearing, picking up speed, and getting louder. I widened my stance and grabbed my dagger, ready for whoever was coming.

A small gasp filled the air as a woman wearing a fur cloak with its hood up stepped in front of me. It was the same cloak one of Talia's ladies had been wearing. She raised her hands, which caused me to tighten my grip on the dagger.

I released my breath when she pushed her hood back. "Talia."

"Raph."

She ran the remaining distance and threw herself into me. I secured my arms around her, feeling her heart hammer against my chest. I breathed her in and felt her body relax.

"We aren't safe yet," I muttered, then pulled away. I stopped when her eyes found mine and tears streamed down her cheeks.

She nodded, wiping them away.

"Gil and Jules are waiting," I said, blinking myself back to reality.

"Jules?"

"Yes," I confirmed, leading the way out.

"How is that possible?"

I glanced over my shoulder. "Later." She pressed her lips together with a dip of her head.

We had one more turn before we would be out of the maze and then all that was left would be to climb over the wall. Breaking through the hedge opening, I jammed my feet into the ground, stopping. Talia slammed into my back.

"Stay behind me," I commanded as the King's Wraith unsheathed his sword in front of us.

Talia

Kasper stood in front of us, sword drawn. I stumbled back. Raph stepped away from me and drew his sword.

"I've been waiting for this," Kasper snarled, lifting his sword.

"Getting beat once wasn't enough?" Raph taunted.

"We will see what you can do without that ragtag group of yours." They circled each other. "I guess I have you to thank for stealing from my father?"

"Those women were never his!" Raph made the first move. Their swords clashed.

No matter how much I hoped for Raph to be the better swordsman, they seemed evenly matched. We wouldn't have long before more guards arrived, and we would be outnumbered. I needed to help.

"Go!" Raph ordered, but I couldn't leave him. Not knowing what else to do, I took off the heeled shoes they had put me in and chucked one of them at Kasper's head. And missed. As I pulled my arm back to throw the other one, a hand grabbed my wrist, and I let out a scream.

A guard yanked me against his chest while five others stepped out behind him.

"Raph!"

His eyes flicked to me. And for a moment, he let all of his walls down, showing me the true pain and fear he carried. My stomach plummeted when he threw his sword at Kasper's feet.

"Don't hurt her." His eyes stayed fixed on me.

"No problem," Prince Kasper replied as he swung his sword straight at Raph's head.

"No!"

Raph didn't flinch or try to move. I fought the guard restraining me as Raph fell to the ground, unconscious.

CHAPTER 35

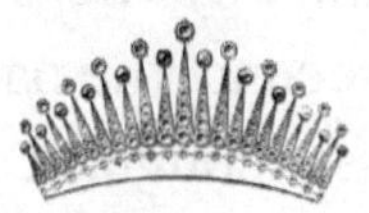

Jules

"You reek." I gagged and covered my nose with my cloak.

"It's not my fault. Raph never told me not to touch the stuff." Gil rubbed his hands on his pants as he came and stood next to me.

"He literally said to be careful because the smell will last for days." I rolled my eyes as I leaned against the brick wall.

"I was. I made sure to put the powder on things that couldn't be thrown away. And it worked."

"They're moving it outside?"

"Yes. I heard the order when I snuck out."

"Now it's up to Raph and Tals," I said, biting the inside of my thumbnail.

"Anything happen out here?" he asked.

"No. The guards are walking the perimeter on the other side of this wall. We are good to wait here."

"Great. Want to go grab some food while we wait?"

I pushed off the wall and stared at him.

"What?" he shrugged.

"First, I'm not going anywhere with you when you smell like that. And second, the party will start soon."

"Okay, no food. Just thought it would help pass the time."

He leaned against the wall next to me. The shadows around us darkened as we waited for Raph and Tals. I fidgeted in the dress Gil and Raph said I had to wear. Gil and I were pretending to be nobles, to help ward off any unwanted attention. But that also meant I couldn't bring my bow, and I felt completely exposed without it.

"Want to play a game?" Gil asked after he finished making marks in the ground with his foot.

I peered at him from the corner of my eye. "What game?"

"How about we get to know each other better? You tell me three things about yourself, but one of them has to be a lie. Then the other person has to guess which one is the lie. I used to play this all the time growing up." His eyes danced with excitement as he explained the game.

"Sure. I'll go first." Folding my arms across my chest I thought of my three things. "One, I don't have siblings.

Two, my favorite time of year is autumn. And three, I don't like games."

Gil stared at me, focusing intently on my eyes as if trying to read my mind.

"The second one is a lie." He leaned back with a lift of his chin.

"Good guess. Your turn."

"It wasn't that hard. I know from experience how competitive you are," he said with a smirk. I narrowed my eyes at him. "And you seem more like a spring person."

"Why's that?"

"You like new beginnings and rainy days."

My lips parted as heat bloomed in my chest.

"My turn. One, I love horses. Two, I never say no to a party. Three, I'm glad you're here." His smile deepened as he dipped his head.

"The first one." I shook my head, pursing my lips. "You don't know how to turn it off, do you?"

"What do you mean? I meant that."

"Sure."

Our eyes widened as the sound of clashing metal rang over the wall.

"Give me a boost," I said, turning to the wall and placing my foot in Gil's hand so he could lift me to see over the top.

It was dark, but I could see two figures in the distance battling it out. A group of people stood further back, holding onto someone. But something about one of the figures fighting caught my attention. My throat closed up. It couldn't be him.

"What's happening?" Gil shouted from below.

My feet slammed into the ground as he brought me down. I couldn't get my mouth to work. I reached for my chest as my heart beat frantically.

"Jules, are you okay? What did you see?" Gil's worried face came into view.

Forcing myself to take a breath I answered, "Raph's fighting my ki...someone, and they have Tals. We need to help." Facing the wall again, I lifted up my foot. "I'll go first and then help you up."

I turned around when I didn't feel Gil's hand.

"How many were there?"

"Why does that matter? Let's go!"

"Think this through. If we were to get captured too, how does that help Talia or Raph?"

"This is our chance!"

"How many?" Gil demanded.

"I don't know, besides the one fighting Raph, maybe six."

"We can't risk it."

"No," I screamed, placing my foot against the wall to jump up.

"Jules, stop. You don't have any experience fighting without your bow. And I'm pretty sure Raph is battling it out with the prince," I froze, "which means it would be me against the other five." His eyes pleaded with me to understand.

"But...I can't," my voice broke.

"We aren't giving up. Adira and Eitan should arrive tomorrow, and we will find another way to save them."

I hung my head, not able to look at him.

When we could no longer hear anything, he lifted me to check over the wall. The space was vacant.

"We will save them," he said, helping me back down.

"How?"

He bit his lip as he rubbed his chin. "What would Raph do?" he muttered to himself before his eyes lit up. "Follow me." He took off down the narrow road.

"Where are we going?"

"To find us some Shades."

CHAPTER 36

Talia

"WHAT ARE YOU GOING to do with him?" I demanded as I tried to match Kasper's pace through the halls of the palace. He had made me ride in a separate carriage with three guards while he took Raph. Relief flooded me when I saw Raph being dragged from the carriage, alive and conscious. However, they had quickly knocked him out again. Two guards then dragged him behind us.

"Please." I reached out to grab Kasper's arm. He stopped outside the doors I knew too well. "I will do anything," I begged. "Please."

"I warned you." His voice was barely above a whisper. He shook my hand off. In one quick movement, he swung open both of the doors, giving me a clear view of King Madden upon his throne.

"How disappointing," the king said, dragging out his words. "I expected more from you, Little Fawn." His words were slow and even, but his eyes were manic.

I leaned back, thinking he would jump off his throne at any moment to attack.

"Wake him up," he commanded.

I flinched as one of the guards slapped Raph across the face.

He regained consciousness, and his piercing green eyes searched for me. Everything inside me shattered.

King Madden's heavy steps echoed through the room, but I couldn't take my eyes off Raph. "Eventually you'll tell me everything. If you'd rather this be painless, I would recommend you be forthcoming right away," King Madden said as he adjusted the rings on his fingers.

Raph didn't respond, he just continued to stare at me.

"The silent type? They are my favorite." The king finished with a backhand across Raph's face, leaving him with a busted lip. "Do you lead the Northern Rebels?"

Silence.

Smack.

Raph's face gained an indent of one of the king's rings. The taste of bile filled my mouth. I couldn't handle it. Every time the king hit Raph, he continued to stare at me, which seemed to enrage King Madden even more.

"What do you want with her?" the king yelled, then kicked Raph in the stomach before he could answer.

"Stop!" I screamed. "Please, stop it!" My cries were futile. They only seemed to stoke the fire inside of the king as he kicked Raph. The look in the king's eyes was pure rage. Rage for blood. "I will do anything. Stop hurting him!"

The room went silent at my plea. King Madden peered over his shoulder with a villainous smile, and he stepped toward me.

"Don't," Raph wheezed.

"There may be an advantage to not killing him if it keeps you in line." King Madden grabbed a lock of my hair and twirled it around his finger.

"You have to promise me you won't hurt him. You must let him live!" The words came out in a rush.

"I don't make promises," he scoffed, and his hand dropped away. "However, as long as you follow my orders, I see no need to dispose of him. But know, the moment you step out of line, his usefulness will no longer exist."

My throat burned as I attempted to swallow the sobs that wanted to break through. I would survive whatever the king threw at me if it meant keeping Raph alive.

I nodded.

"I, of course, will have to test your obedience," he stated, turning back to his throne "The party tonight was cut short, and to make it up to everyone, I have decided to throw something even bigger tomorrow night."

I followed his gaze to Prince Kasper whose brow was furrowed in confusion.

Finally, the king looked to us. "A wedding."

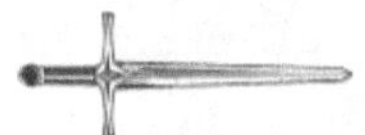

"Your Highness, is there anything we can do?" Catherine's voice was soft and gentle, mimicking the strokes she made while brushing out my hair.

I hadn't said anything since being locked back up. There was too much to tell to even know where to start, and every time I opened my mouth, I saw Raph's bloody, broken body. How could I have allowed myself to believe that I could escape?

A sob broke out and I shook. "Oh, Princess." Catherine dropped the brush and wrapped me in her arms. "It will be okay. Everything will be okay."

Her words made me cry harder. She was wrong, nothing was okay, and there was no way to fix it. I'm not sure how long I sat there crying into Catherine's arms, but at some point, the tears dried up and my breathing settled.

"I'm sorry—"

"Don't," Malenee interrupted, startling me. I hadn't noticed her come over. "You have every right to feel the way you do and more." She kneeled in front of me.

I wiped the remaining tears from my eyes. "Thank you. Both of you," I said, reaching out to grab their hands, "for everything." They squeezed mine in response.

"Your Highness..." Catherine sent Malenee a look before continuing, "We want you to know if there is *anything* you need from us. We will do it."

The emphasis she put on anything made me think she was trying to send me a hidden message, but there was nothing they could do for me unless they knew of some way to free Raph and sneak him out of the palace, which was impossible. Guards would be all over the place after what had happened, and the king warned me he would be watching my every move until the wedding.

"It's hopeless," I said, dropping my head into my hands. "Not only am I getting married to the King's Wraith tomorrow, but King Madden has my friend locked away, ready to kill him, if I put one toe out of line. Oh," I said, throwing my head up, "and King Madden has the journal."

"What?" Malenee asked.

"That's why he stopped by. He knew I had the journal. Someone had taken it from this room."

"Who?" Catherine asked.

"I'd bet my freedom it was Celeste."

"What did he do to you?" Malenee's brows drew to-gether.

I tried to form the words, but I couldn't get myself to share what he had confessed. "He only threatened me, saying if I were to ever speak about the journal to anyone, he would show me how cruel he could be."

Catherine shivered as Malenee stared at the floor.

"It's the key to stopping him. I know it."

"What about your friend? Were there others with him?" Catherine asked.

"Yes, they were waiting for us."

"Maybe they—" Catherine started.

"No." I allowed my shoulders to slump. "There's no way they'll be able to get in. Not unless the palace has a secret entrance."

"Your Highness!" Malenee finally broke her stare.

"Yes?"

"There is one!"

"What?"

"Where?" Catherine chimed in, looking confused.

"It is an old escape route, only the late king and his captain knew about it."

"How do you know about it then?"

"Gale told me about it."

Catherine's eyebrows lifted as if it made perfect sense.

"Who's Gale?"

"I'll let Malenee answer that one." Catherine smirked.

Malenee wrung her hands together. "He is a part of the King's Guard. But he doesn't hold any loyalty to the king. He is the one who told us about the Northern Rebels."

"And..." Catherine added.

"And...we have been seeing each other for the past couple of months," she gushed, dipping her chin.

I was not expecting that. If anyone would have had a thing with one of the guards, I would have put my money on Catherine.

"You've seen the passage before?"

"Not entirely, Your Highness. I've only seen the door that leads to the passageway."

Rubbing my temples, I paced the room. It didn't change anything unless we figured out a way to inform Gil and Jules of the passageway, but who knew if they would get the message in time. No. I couldn't depend on them. I needed to figure out a way to free Raph by myself and escape.

"Does Gale have access to the dungeon?" I asked, trying to formulate some sort of plan in my head.

"Yes. What are you thinking, Your Highness?"

"I'm not sure yet, but if I can find a way to escape my guards before the wedding and if you guys could break Raph out, maybe we could use the secret passageway and escape." They both stared at me. "It's a lot of ifs." I twisted the fabric of my nightgown in my hands, trying to release some of the tension inside me.

"We would need to distract the guards in the dungeon and the ones watching you," Malenee stated.

What I wouldn't do for some of Mother's tonic. She had one that could calm a horse down. Then maybe I could think straight.

I dropped the fabric. "How well stocked is the kitchen?"

"King Madden makes sure they have every option available for him." Malenee answered with a tilt to her head.

"I have an idea. I'll need ingredients from the kitchen and maybe the palace's Healer. Is that possible?"

They both looked at me, then each other, and back at me.

Malenee spoke first. "Your Highness, the moment we found out that an heir from the line of the late king and queen lived, we were given a sense of hope."

"Hope?" I lifted my shoulders.

"Yes. Hope that things could change, that King Madden would no longer be king, and that we could be free. It has spread like wildfire to everyone who works in the palace and even some of the King's Guard. There are many who would do anything to help," she added.

"I can't dethrone the king. I'm only planning my escape. I can't save them." My throat constricted.

"We know you can't do this on your own," Malenee said, and Catherine placed her hand on my knee. "But we do believe you are the sign of change, and we aren't alone in that. The Northern Rebels will help you."

"King Madden asked Raph if he was a part of that group," I added. If my seven strangers were a part of that group, it would answer a lot of questions about their secrecy. "I think he might be."

"Write down the ingredients you need, Your Highness. We will do the rest." Malenee walked over to the desk and withdrew a piece of paper. I followed and jotted down every ingredient, thankful that Mother constantly made me recite recipes to her.

The moment I handed the paper to Malenee, a sharp knock echoed throughout the room causing us all to jump. Malenee gave me a nod before she walked over to the door. Catherine went to the windows and closed the curtains. Malenee opened the door, and Mistress Pennier's stern face scoured the room before she found me.

"You two are dismissed," she said matter-of-factly.

I was about to open my mouth and tell her that she didn't have the right to dismiss them when Catherine walked by gently shaking her head. They bowed before walking out. The moment they crossed the threshold, Mistress Pennier shut the door.

She turned to me, holding a small black box in front of her. "I have something for you, Your Highness."

"What is it?"

"A wedding gift." Her words made my stomach churn.

"I'm quite tired."

"It won't take long, Your Highness." Her mouth opened but then closed again. Whatever she had to say was making her nervous. "It's from his Royal Highness, Prince Kasper."

I wanted to tell her to take it back and that I didn't want anything from him, but she stood upright, extending the box to me. She wouldn't leave unless I accepted it.

"You can put it there," I said, pointing to the vanity.

"This may not be easy for you," she started.

I scoffed in response.

She pinned me with her signature stern look and placed the gift down. "But you're not the only one who doesn't have a choice in the matter."

Bowing, she briskly walked out of the room.

Ignoring her comment and the black box, I made my way to the fire and curled up in a chair. I hugged my knees to my chest going over every detail about how the escape plan would go. Losing focus, my eyes closed.

I jolted awake and uncurled myself, heading toward the bed. My treacherous eyes landed on the black box as I passed it. Curiosity got the better of me, and I opened the lid. A small piece of parchment lay folded on top.

Princess Talia,

I can't give you what you want, but I hope by returning this, you will find the strength to face tomorrow.

Prince Kasper

Under the note lay a dagger, the one Raph had given me. The moment my fingers touched the hilt, a sense of safety wrapped around me. A single tear fell onto the blade as I stared at the inscription carved into it, still unsure of what it meant.

I held it close and moved to the bed where I placed it gently under my pillow. I fell asleep with a new sense of comfort.

CHAPTER 37

Raph

"HOPE YOU LIKE YOUR new accommodation, because you won't see anything outside of these four walls again," one of the guards snickered as he threw me into the cell.

A cough ricocheted up my body, causing me to spit up blood. I'd been on the receiving end of worse beatings, but that one had cut it close. I crawled over to the wall and propped myself against the cold, damp stone. A groan escaped me when I confirmed how many ribs I had broken. It at least distracted me from the radiating ache coming from my head thanks to the prince. I planned on returning the favor the next time I saw him.

Tipping my head back, I wondered if Talia knew that the prince was Jules's kidnapper. Her pale face, stricken with fear, flashed before my eyes. She shouldn't have made that deal. My muscles tightened. But the wedding was inevitable. Especially after I failed her. No doubt, Jules and Gil would've guessed what happened, but there was nothing they could do before tomorrow.

Why had Alon let her return to Gasmere, if he knew? I thought back to the unexpected communications Alon began with the Kingdom of Nefali, to Nadav and Hafsa showing up shortly after. It was all so obvious. Maybe things would've been different if I had pieced it together sooner, but my disbelief in the lost princess had blinded me.

"Pay up," one of the guards shouted from outside the door. The guards were playing some sort of gambling game, most likely Tutten. It was the locals' favorite and the sound of dice hitting the table gave it away. Taking a deep breath, I closed my eyes. How was I going to save her?

In the end, exhaustion took me before I could come up with a halfway decent plan.

Talia

"There," I said, adding in the last ingredient. Malenee handed me three small vials to put the powder in. "I increased the potency. A small pinch is all it will take."

"This will knock them out long enough?" Malenee asked as I handed her one of them.

"Yes, they will be out for at least an hour."

"Wow, it's like magic." Catherine held up her vial into the sunlight.

"The closest thing to it." I placed the third vial in a small pocket Catherine had made in my chemise.

"What is that one for, Your Highness?" Malenee asked.

"Insurance."

"Smart." She placed hers in her skirt's pocket.

"I'm up first." Giving a bow, Catherine took her leave.

"We should finish," Malenee spoke softly. "Just in case."

Dipping my chin, I collected the leftover ingredients together. A small white berry rolled to the end of the desk. I hesitated to pick it up. It was what dampened the potency of the sleeping powder, the antidote. I placed it in the same pocket as the vial.

After checking that no evidence was left, I followed Malenee to the vanity. I still needed to look like I was going through with the wedding.

"It will work," I said, feeling Malenee's hand shaking as she tried to place a pin in my hair.

"Yes, Your Highness. Shouldn't she be back already?"

I had the same thought a few moments ago. "She will be back soon."

The door opened. Catherine shut it quickly, and briskly walked over to us.

"It's done."

Malenee and I released a breath at the same time.

"Perfect. All we have to do is wait for a couple of minutes for it to kick in."

"I will meet up with Gale in the dungeons, and we will meet you and Catherine at the passage's entrance."

"Yes."

"I can't believe this is working!" Catherine placed her hands on her face.

"Princess Talia," Mistress Pennier's voice called from the other side of the door.

"What is she doing here?" I asked in a harsh whisper.

Panic was written on all of our faces.

"It's okay. She probably wants to check in," Malenee stated calmly. "Catherine, go grab the dress."

Catherine ran to the closet as Malenee walked to the door.

"It's a good thing I decided to come by, Your Highness," Mistress Pennier said with a bow. "I had to dismiss your guards. They were both half asleep." She clicked her tongue with disapproval.

Malenee gave me a panicked look behind Mistress Pennier's shoulder.

I cleared my throat. "Thank you."

"Why aren't you dressed yet, Your Highness?"

"We were about to, Ma'am," Catherine said, carrying a dress that swallowed her whole body.

"Hurry up, girls. There isn't much time."

At her order, Catherine and Malenee helped get me into the ivory satin dress.

"Yes. That will do." Mistress Pennier rubbed her chin. "Excuse me, Your Highness, but I must see to some other duties." She gave a small bow. "Someone will be here shortly to escort you down."

I dipped my head, not trusting my voice to speak. My whole body was shaking. The moment she shut the door, I let out a groan.

"What are we going to do?" Malenee asked.

"It's all ruined!" Catherine moaned.

"No. It's okay. We have more powder," I said, patting my pocket. "We will give it to the new guards. Malenee, go meet up with Gale. He is probably getting worried. Follow the plan as before. Catherine, I need you to go get some more drinks for the new guards." I reached into my pocket and handed her the vial.

They nodded but didn't move.

"Now," I ordered.

"Yes, Your Highness." Catherine bowed, followed by Malenee.

"Of course, Your Highness."

They left in a flurry. I paced the room, waiting for Catherine to return.

I jumped when a loud knock filled the room. "Princess Talia," a deep voice said.

I opened the door and two guards stood shoulder to shoulder staring at me.

"We are here to escort you." The one on the left said.

"But my maid hasn't returned."

"I'm sorry, Your Highness, but King Madden gave us the order to come and get you straight away."

I searched for Catherine and sweat dripped down my back as I tried to come up with something.

"Princess?" The one on the right spoke.

"I...I need to..." Their eyebrows lifted at the same time. "Relieve myself." I blurted out.

Their eyes widened.

"Of course, Your Highness."

"But I can't do it by myself." I gestured to the large skirt that surrounded my hips.

"Right," the one on the right gulped. "I will go get you some assistance."

"Your Highness," Catherine's voice echoed from down the hall.

The guard's shoulders relaxed.

"I require your assistance."

Catherine bowed, then followed me into the room.

"What happened?" She held two mugs in her hands.

"They came to get me, so I had to waste time until you got back. I told them I had to relieve myself."

Catherine tried to cover her mouth with one of her hands as she smiled. "What do we do?"

"I don't know."

"We could still give it to them."

"No, the king is expecting me. He will send more guards soon if I don't leave." I rubbed the back of my neck.

"There has to be another way. There's some left. Is there someone else we could give it to?"

I bit down on my lip.

"Prince Kasper," I gushed.

"Really?"

"No, this will work. Have you heard about the Blood Chalice?"

"Yes," Catherine answered, scrunching up her nose.

"We need to put the powder in that."

"But you must drink that too."

"Your Highness, we really must go." One of the guards said through the door.

"Catherine, do it. Trust me."

CHAPTER 38

Talia

With every step that echoed across the white stone floor, I tried to calm my racing heart. I didn't take in any of the faces that stared directly at me. I couldn't. All I could do was run through the plan over and over, praying that it would work. There were so many variables that could go wrong.

The soft melody in the background anchored me to my surroundings. Red rose petals covered the aisle I was walking down. Faint whispers could be heard from the people who stood on either side of me. And up ahead, on the dais, stood King Madden and Prince Kasper, waiting for me. The skirts of my dress swished with every step I took, but all I could feel was that small white berry pressed against my hip.

Prince Kasper met me at the base, offering his arm to assist me up the steps. The air in the room became thin as King Madden stared at me, a sinister grin claiming his face. I shifted my gaze from where he sat on his throne to a small golden pedestal with a gold bowl on top. It stood between Kasper and me.

King Madden stood. Silence fell.

"Good people of Landore, what a momentous occasion this is." His voice was strong and exuberant as it echoed across the room. "Tonight, our kingdom shall find peace in the union of Prince Kasper and Princess Talia." Cheers echoed throughout the room, but my eyes could not leave the bowl in front of me. My throat tightened as King Madden extended a hand out to me. The look from Kasper told me I had to take it. Reaching out, I accepted his hand. He brought me to the edge of the dais.

"Princess Talia has been lost to us for over eighteen years. Because of this, she was never able to claim her true calling. Although it's later than I planned, a ceremony will be held for her tonight, declaring her new position in this world as Princess Talia of Landore."

Another set of cheers rang out, and King Madden led me back to the gold bowl. I peered inside, and my breath caught. My reflection was tinted black.

King Madden spoke again. "Thirty years ago, I instilled the callings to bring peace and order to our kingdom, to give people a sense of purpose and belonging…" Those were the last things that it did. They had segregated Landore and caused division and economic hardships for many villages. "As king I embody the callings, and now it's time for Princess Talia to do the same."

Off to the side, an older man adorned in white robes walked up the platform and came to stand next to me. His aged eyes searched my face, and for a moment, I saw pain cross his weathered face, but it didn't stay. My heart pounded inside my chest.

The old man cleared his throat. "Tonight, Princess Talia will embody all of the callings by dipping her fingers into the bowl that represents the colors of each calling. From this night forward she will forever represent the five callings." He stretched his arm out toward the bowl, waiting for me to do my part.

I hovered my fingers over the surface of the gold bowl. Its mirror image looked as though she was reaching for me. I needed to dip my fingers in, stain them. Mark myself as a fraud, so he could claim me as his.

The heat from King Madden's stare seared my back. I couldn't delay any longer. The tips of my fingers touched the cool dye and a part of me died as he took another thing from me. King Madden grabbed my left wrist and raised my black tinted fingers for all to see. Everyone let out a cry of approval.

"You're mine, Little Fawn," his voice was low so only I heard.

Dropping my wrist, he sauntered back to his throne. The bowl and pedestal were removed, and Kasper filled its place. My focus stayed on my stained fingers as the old man spoke again, "This bond, once made, shall never be broken..." His words faded in and out.

Movement behind the prince caught my eye. A young boy was walking up the steps carrying a chalice with both hands.

"Your Highness." The older man gestured for me to take the chalice.

Reaching out, I accepted it with both hands. I had no clue if Catherine had been successful or not because the powder had no color or odor. My eyes flicked to Prince Kasper. He stood looking very much like a prince in his crimson jacket with the same gold overlay as my dress. He stared back, but his face was stoic, not letting any emotion sneak out. He was much larger than me, which meant the powder would take longer to take effect on him.

Bringing the chalice to my lips, I let the liquid barely kiss them before faking a swallow. The old man grabbed it from me and placed it in the prince's hands. Without any hesitation, he brought it to his lips and took a deep drink.

I looked out to the people as the old man continued to speak. The oval ballroom was filled. I recognized a handful from the recent parties. My ladies were sitting in the front row. When they noticed my stare, their faces lit up, and they waved—except for Celeste. She sat like a statue, not giving anything away. But before I looked away, her stare found me, filled with rage.

Prince Kasper's voice drew me back. "I, Prince Kasper, give to you..." his words faltered for a moment "Princess Talia, my body, soul, and mind. From this moment on, we shall never be separated."

His weight shifted slightly as he tried to blink away the effects of the powder.

"If you will now repeat the same vow, Your Highness."

"I..." I said while Kasper shook his head as his eyelids closed partly. "Princess Talia, give to you—"

Thud.

Moving before the first scream let out, I grabbed my skirts and ran down the side of the dais. Finding my way behind the curtains as my vision blurred. Catherine must have used more than a pinch. Reaching into my skirts, I pulled out the berry and threw it into my mouth.

"Get her!" King Madden's shout rose above the cries.

My eyes landed on the door, and for the first time I realized that it could be locked. Not wasting time to dwell on it, I grabbed the handle and pushed with all my might.

The door sprung open, catapulting me to the floor.

"Your Highness!" Catherine's hand grabbed my arm, helping me stand.

"They're coming," I rasped. I felt weak, but the berry had corrected my vision.

Wrapping her arm around my waist, we ran down the hall together. Catherine kept her arm around me as she opened a door to our left. The sound of heavy boots caused us both to look over our shoulders.

A mass of red was making its way toward us.

"Go," Catherine yelled, pushing me through the door.

Raph

I awoke with a start and sleepily glanced around in the fading light. It took me a moment to realize what had changed was the lack of noise.

I sat up straighter at the sound of light shuffling across stone. Hopping up, ignoring the head rush I felt, I quietly made my way to the corner. The footsteps fell silent outside my door but were replaced with the jingle of keys.

The door to my prison creaked open and a woman's head popped into my view.

"We need to hurry. Can you walk by yourself?" She asked, then fully opened the door.

"Who are you?" She was tall, with dark features. Nothing about her was recognizable.

"I'm one of Princess Talia's maids. I'm here to get you out."

"Forget about me," I argued. "You need to get her out. I have friends staying at the Lucky Lion in town. She'll be safe with them."

"Don't worry, the princess is safe. She is waiting for us." She glanced over her shoulder as if she was expecting someone to come in and join us. "We need to hurry."

I followed behind her, down the hall they had dragged me through. When we approached the end, the sound of deep breathing grew louder. Three guards were passed out face first on a table with coins and dice lying about. I gave her a quizzical look.

"That wasn't me." She gave a short laugh. "You have Her Highness to thank for that. And I believe these belong to you." She grabbed a pile off a small table—my weapons. I fastened the harness around my chest and waist, then sheathed my sword.

Another guard stepped out from around the corner. I drew my sword.

"Stop!" She stepped in front of me. "He's here to help."

The guard lifted his hands in surrender. His eyes stayed on me as he grabbed his own hand in front of his chest and gave it a shake—the Aydencian sign.

"Gale?" I had never met the spy who was planted in the King's Guard, all I knew was a name.

He nodded.

I extended out my arm, and he grabbed onto my forearm. "Nice to finally meet you."

"We need to move," Talia's maid said as she bounced from one foot to the other.

"Be safe," Gale said to her while releasing my arm.

"You're not coming?" I asked.

"I'll stay back to make sure no one follows."

Dipping my chin, I moved to follow Talia's maid down a dim hallway. Eventually we reached a door that led into a tunnel. She must be using the servant's passageways.

As I fought through the pain every step emitted through my body, I focused on Talia and how she was the one doing the rescuing. Within a month she had won over the king's staff, and they were willing to risk their safety to free her. I wasn't surprised though. She had done the same thing to us. As if hearing my thoughts, the maid glanced over her shoulder to check on me. Our slow pace was making her anxious. But I couldn't move any faster with my injuries.

"We're almost there." Her words were laced with worry as her eyes danced from my busted lip to my swollen eye.

She wasn't lying. After a few hundred feet, she stopped at a door. She knocked in sequences and waited for a response.

The door swung open, and there was another young woman standing on the other side wearing the same outfit, but she was much shorter and had red hair. The hairs on my neck stood at the feeling of familiarity.

"Finally!" The redhead grabbed the arm of the other. "I was worried that the powder hadn't worked. We need to hurry. They will be searching all over for her." The redhead's eyes landed on me, squinting together before she shook her head.

They walked further into the room, and I followed behind slowly, unsure of where they were leading me. I looked past what seemed to be a supply room for signs of Talia. "Where is she? You said she would meet us."

Neither of them answered me, but the taller one I had followed moved to the far wall where she knocked on the stone. After a couple of knocks the sound changed. It was hollower. She gave it a shove, but nothing happened. Peering over her shoulder, the redhead went over to join her. Together they counted down, then shoved the wall with their body weight. A crack became visible between the stones. They continued to push until the gap was big enough for someone to walk through.

"It's safe, Your Highness. You can come out," the red-head spoke into the darkened passageway.

I relaxed briefly when Talia stepped out. When I took in her appearance, my whole body went rigid. There was no describing how she looked, other than other-worldly.

"Raph!" She ran the remaining distance to me, stopping abruptly when she took in my state. "You look awful!"

A deep chuckle rumbled through my chest. "It's good to see you too, Princess." She flinched at my words but tried to cover it up.

"I'm sorry…" She reached out to touch my arm.

My eyes widened as I took in her black tipped fingers. She retracted her hand, hiding it behind her back.

"You have nothing to apologize for," I said, seeing the pain in her eyes.

"Ahem…" one of them interrupted.

"I'm sorry, but we need to hurry. They will be looking for you," the other added.

"Right." Talia created more distance between us, and it took everything in me not to reach out to her.

"This will lead out of the palace," the taller one stated to me and Talia.

"Wait." Talia grabbed the girl's forearm. "The plan was for you two to come with us. I can't…I won't leave you here."

"Your Highness, I'm sorry, but we were never going to leave with you," She placed her hand over Talia's. The redhead walked over and grabbed her other hand.

"If we left with you, King Madden would know it was an inside job. He would punish every servant until someone confessed who helped you escape. We can't put them through that. We have to stay."

Placing a reassuring hand on the hilt of the sword I'd taken, I watched as Talia battled her thoughts. Her eyes flicked to my face before she wrapped her arms around both of them.

"I will come back for you. For all of you," she promised.

The two women nodded and tightened their grips.

"This belongs with you." The taller one pulled out a small book from her apron.

"How? What did you do?" Talia's eyes grew wide as she clutched onto the book.

"It doesn't matter. Go be the hope that Landore needs!" They pushed her toward the opening with me following after.

The passageway was dark and wet. It smelled as if we were surrounded by dirt rather than stone. Before they closed the door on us, Talia pushed past me to reach back out to them.

"We'll be okay," one of them whispered into the small crack, before blackness took over. I couldn't hear or see anything besides Talia's irregular breathing.

"We need to keep moving," I said more as a demand than a suggestion. For her maids were right. Talia was the symbol of hope, but not just for Landore.

CHAPTER 39

Talia

I WALKED DOWN THE dark passageway, keeping one hand on the damp wall and the other clutching the queen's journal. Having it in my hands gave me a new sense of strength.

"Let me lead," Raph's raspy voice was closer than I'd expected, sending my heart fluttering. His hand grazed my back, and he trailed it down to find my hand. All of a sudden it seemed as though there wasn't enough air in the tunnel for both of us.

Our pace was slow. There were no noises outside of our labored breathing and the echoes of our steps. I had so much I wanted to say, but I didn't know where to start. I couldn't help but wonder if there was any truth behind his last letter.

"Poison, huh?" he whispered.

"It wasn't poison, just a sleeping powder."

"It was definitely effective. Remind me not to get on your bad side." A laugh traced his words.

"Thank you."

"For what?"

"For coming to rescue me. I don't know how you figured out I was here but thank you." I squeezed his hand.

"I fail to see the part where I rescued you. From where I'm standing, you're the one who did the rescuing."

"But you still came."

"Always, Your Highness."

I pulled back at his words, feeling a divide between us. We returned to silence.

The air around us changed. It became less dense and tasted almost salty. I saw Raph's silhouette in front of me. Peering past him, I noticed a set of stairs leading upward.

"Stay here for a moment," he said while climbing the stairs.

I wanted to argue, but he left before I could. I didn't like the idea of being separated. For a moment, I thought I could hear footsteps behind me. I edged closer to the stairs ready to run up them if Raph didn't return soon.

"There's a way out," Raph's voice startled me. He descended the final step. "But it's going to take a while to dig our way out."

"Dig?"

"The way out has been sealed with stones, but some of them have crumbled away. I think we can hack our way out," he said, sounding optimistic.

"I guess we have no other choice."

I followed him but kept glancing over my shoulder, unable to shake the feeling that someone was behind us. When we reached the top, there was a wall of stones taller than me stacked on top of each other. There were small gaps between some of them where the light from the setting sun shone through.

"Here, use this to dig around them." Raph handed me one of his daggers.

"I'm good. I still have the one you gave me," I said, reaching under my skirts to pull it out. When I straightened up, I found him giving me a strange look. But he turned away before I could decipher it and began to hack at the wall.

I glanced back down the stairs again. The noise coming from his efforts was louder than I liked. I sucked in a breath and turned toward the wall to hack with vigor.

Beads of sweat trickled down my back and my arm burned. Raph had managed to get two stones loose, and I was almost done with one, but at that rate, it would take us hours to get a hole big enough to fit through. I was mid-strike when Raph suddenly grabbed my arm, stopping me. He put his hand holding the dagger to his mouth, signaling me to be silent.

I strained my ears to try and hear whatever it was he had heard, ignoring the chills rippling through me. I turned my head toward the stairs, expecting to hear something. Instead, the sound was coming from the other side of the wall.

Raph pushed me so my back was against the stones and we were no longer standing in front of the small openings. His arm stretched across my stomach as he pressed himself against the wall as well.

"This has to be it," a man rasped from the other side.

"Let me look at the map. We don't have time to be wrong," a woman whispered back.

"Look, someone has already gotten started for us," a different man with a lighter voice said.

Raph and I made eye contact. We pushed ourselves from the wall and saw two playful, amber eyes staring back at us.

"No way!" Gil's face came into view as he stepped back. "This job just got a lot easier," he said over his shoulder.

"What do you mean?"

"Look for yourself," Gil stepped back with a smirk.

Adira came into view, her eyes growing wide. "Talia! Raph! What in Landore?"

"Tals!" Jules's voice broke through the hole.

"Jules! How did you find us?"

"It was Alon, Hafsa, and Nadav. They sent us this map." Gil said from somewhere behind Jules.

"What map?" I asked.

"We'll have time to discuss this later. We need to get out," Raph said through his teeth.

"Right. Now comes the fun part." Gil's gleeful tone had me look at Raph nervously. "Stand back you two. Oh, and cover your ears."

Raph must have understood what was about to happen because he instantly led me down a couple of steps, keeping his arm wrapped around me. He turned us so his back faced the opening.

BOOM.

The walls shook and my ears rang. It felt like the ball all over again. I would have fallen to the ground if Raph hadn't been holding me up. After a few moments, he released his hold on me. I coughed as dust and debris littered the air around us. When it cleared, I could see the opening again. It was now three times the size of what it was before.

I stepped forward, eager to get to Jules when I was lifted off the ground. I was about to demand Raph put me down, but the sound of a stampede of feet echoed from the darkness behind us.

"Take her," Raph yelped as he pushed me through the hole, and two hands grabbed underneath my arms.

"Eitan," I said on an exhale, relieved when he got me through. I sucked in a breath, and squirmed in his grip. "The guards are coming. We have to get him out!"

"No," Raph barked through the hole. "Eitan, get her out of here. Now!"

Eitan didn't hesitate for a moment as he spun around and sprinted away from Raph.

"What are you doing? Go back! Eitan, put me down this instant." He ignored my commands as he continued running away from the palace. I lifted myself to peer over his shoulder and found Jules and Adira right behind us. Gil was by the opening, and he seemed to be placing something sparking inside.

Another loud boom sounded and dust covered the opening, but before the dust settled, Eitan rounded a corner.

"We can't leave them!"

"Don't worry, Princess. They can handle themselves," Eitan assured.

We headed toward the southern side of the palace, cutting across the back of the palace gardens. Adira sprinted past us and didn't show any signs of slowing down as she approached the cliffside first. I wasn't sure what the plan was, but there was nothing but the hungry waves below us. The black rocky beach was further west of us. Adira grabbed something from the ground, then turned around and fell off the side of the cliff.

I screamed and shoved myself out of Eitan's arms.

I hit the ground more painfully than I anticipated, but I ignored it as I rushed to the edge, praying she didn't fall to her death. My knees nearly buckled when I saw her still alive, gripping onto a rope, and maneuvering herself down. At the bottom, there was a boat with one broad sail wading in the choppy waves away from the black rocks. Adira suddenly let go of the rope, and the water engulfed her.

"Adira!" I yelled.

"It's okay. She is the best swimmer of all of us. She will get to the knarve first and get it ready," Eitan explained.

"So the plan is for us to drown in those angry waves as we try to swim to that boat out there?" I looked at Jules who was just catching up. Neither of us knew how to swim. I scoured the area, looking for another way down, but besides that small opening the cliffside was covered with trees. I couldn't see another way down.

"It's called a knarve, and don't worry, I won't let anything happen to you. It's the quickest way for us to get a clean getaway." Eitan placed his hand on my shoulder before going over to the rope Adira had just used. "I will go first and you can follow after me." He turned his back against the drop off and put tension on the rope. "Jules, remember what we promised." And with that he stepped off the cliff.

"What is Eitan talking about?" I asked Jules, who came to stand next to me. She secured her bow around her back.

"It doesn't matter," she muttered and looked away.

A shout made us turn to look back toward the palace.

The pressure in my chest eased as I saw Gil and Raph in the distance running straight for us. However, not too far behind them were a group of the King's Guard.

"What are you doing? Go! Go!" Raph barked at us when he and Gil were in hearing range.

Gil was the first to reach us, and he explained to me what I must do to descend the cliff. He placed the rope in my hand. I hadn't retained a single word he had said because everything was background noise as I stared into the black waters. I looked over my shoulder to see Raph reach us with his sword drawn. The guards were seconds away. There were about five of them, and King Madden was leading the charge.

"Get her out, now!" Raph roared to Jules as he stood right in front of me in a fighting stance with his sword ready.

"Are you ready to get a little practice in?" Gil joked as he drew his sword, but his voice was tight.

"Try to keep up with me this time." Raph shifted his weight forward as they met the first guards.

I turned to Jules, who had already fitted an arrow.

"Halt!" King Madden yelled at the same time that Jules released. The arrow pierced into the side of a guard's neck. He went down. My eyes widened as I looked to her but she was already drawing back another arrow, unfazed. Raph and Gil were back-to-back in front of us fighting the other four. King Madden stood with his sword drawn, staring at me with malice.

"I can't get a clear shot," Jules complained.

The fighting had pushed us to the cliff's edge. We had nowhere else to go, and Raph and Gil kept losing ground.

Thud.

An arrow lodged into the ground between Jules and me. She shifted her aim. More guards were making their way toward us.

"You can end this," King Madden yelled over the fighting. Another arrow skimmed past Jules. Tightening my grip on the rope, I realized my other hand still clutched the journal. Looking at King Madden's manic expression, I knew what I had to do.

"Stop!" I yelled.

The fighting ceased. Raph and Gil squared off with those they had been fighting while new group stood behind King Madden with their bowstrings drawn back.

"Jules." I pulled her focus to the journal and lifted my chin. She arched her brow but gave me a curt nod. I lifted the journal into the air over the edge. "King Madden. Let me and my friends go, and I'll return what is yours."

He stepped forward, eyeing the journal in my hands. "Don't be foolish, Little Fawn. End this now, and I'll make their deaths quick and painless." His face held no sign of worry, but I knew what I had seen in my room. The journal meant something to him, and that is all I needed.

I tossed the journal into the sky toward the closest tree. Everyone's eyes followed the book and Jules released an arrow pinning the book to the tree.

"Jump!" I turned toward the cliff. I dropped the rope and clutched Jules's hand as we threw ourselves off the cliff's edge.

A deep scream ripped through my lungs as I fell.

The moment I broke into the icy dark water, I was no longer in control of my panic. I couldn't see anything. I had no idea how to break through to the surface, and I no longer held Jules's hand. I frantically moved my arms and legs, trying to get to the top, but my heavy skirts pulled me down. A burning sensation filled my lungs, and I opened my mouth for air only to gulp down salt water instead. I fought against the water, but I couldn't tell which way was up. Then there was nothingness.

CHAPTER 40

Talia

EVERYTHING BURNED WHEN I inhaled. It made me cough. I couldn't stop coughing and spitting up salt water.

"I got you, relax." My back vibrated as Raph spoke into my ear.

"Jules," I croaked.

"Gil's got her," he said with a labored breath. "Hold your breath," he commanded at the same moment an arrow flew past our heads.

Once again, I was submerged in the water. I thrashed. The danger above the surface did nothing to dampen my fear of drowning. Raph's arm across my chest tightened, and I broke through the surface with a gasp. Arrows were flying toward us, and it seemed like we weren't getting any closer to the knarve.

BOOM.

The cliff's edge shook and rocks and debris littered the water.

"What was that?" My throat felt as though someone was racking their nails down it.

"Don't worry about it," Raph's response was labored. "Your dress is slowing us down."

"I know." I felt the pull my dress had as if it yearned to belong to the ocean floor.

"Don't fight me." Raph moved his arm to my waist as he turned me to face him. "I won't let you drown." His eyes pierced through me with that promise.

"Okay."

"Deep breath." He breathed in and out with me. "Hold this one."

The moment I reached the height of the breath, we went back under. My mind screamed at me to fight, to do everything I could to reach the surface. But instead, I forced myself to focus on Raph's touch.

One hand was around my waist until it moved up my side. I almost took a huge gulp of water when his fingers touched the top of my dress and grabbed the fabric tightly. I opened my eyes but slammed them shut again at the burn of the salt water. My heartbeat was erratic, but I couldn't tell if it was from Raph's touch or the fact that I was losing air.

I felt something trail down my side, then pressure around my ribcage released and the dress fell from me.

Once again, Raph's arm encircled me as he brought me back to the surface. I didn't notice any more arrows piercing the water, but I couldn't see anything on top of the cliff from my angle in the water.

"That was extremely reckless." His hot breath hit my ear. "It's a miracle we survived that fall."

"But it worked."

"You shouldn't have done it." His words were clipped.

"Why are you mad?"

"Grab the rope!" Adira's voice echoed across the water.

My face was sprayed with water as a piece of rope landed inches from me.

"Hold on," Raph said.

We were pulled toward the knarve, which from that view now resembled a large ship.

"Can you climb up?" Eitan asked over the side.

"Yeah," I rasped.

I had lost my shoes at some point, which made it easier to find the carved handholds below the surface. I reached to grab one above me and pulled myself up. When I got close to the top, Eitan's large hands grabbed under my elbows and lifted me the rest of the way.

My legs wobbled on the ship's floor. Eitan kept his arm around me to keep me upright until Adira came over and placed a blanket over me. He walked over to the edge and yelled something to Raph before he and Adira moved around the ship.

I peered up at the cliff, a lone silhouette stood on its edge. The hairs on my arms stood up.

"You're okay!" Jules ran over to me, engulfing me in a hug. But all I could do was watch the dark figure. They showed no sign of pursuit.

Something hit the floor, and I moved my focus. Raph's body was unmoving, but it was the blood pooling around him that had my heart catching in my throat. I fell to my knees and peeled back his shirt to expose a large gash above his hip bone.

"What do we do?" Jules kneeled beside me.

Deeply inhaling through my nose, I begged my mind to focus. I reached under my chemise, thankful that my dagger was still strapped to my thigh. I cut a piece of the fabric and pressed it against the cut.

"Put pressure here," I directed Jules.

A moan escaped Raph's lips.

I cut another length of fabric, secured it around his waist, and replaced Jules's hands with mine. "Go get Adira," I begged.

She nodded, then hurried away.

"Why didn't you say you were hurt?" I muttered under my breath.

The side of his mouth lifted. "And where...is the fun in that...Princess?"

"Stop talking."

My hands were shaking, but I kept firm pressure against his wound. There was no way I was going to let that infuriatingly stubborn man die.

"What do you need?" Adira appeared with Jules behind her.

"I'm fine," Raph said as he tried to push himself up, which resulted in another groan and him falling back down.

"Don't move!" I looked to Adira, "Do you have any supplies? Needles? Thread?"

"No, all we have are some rags and alcohol." She shook her head, and her wet hair smacked across her eyes.

"That's better than nothing, but he will need to be stitched up. We will have to find the nearest village to get supplies." His eyes had closed. "Raph?"

"Is he…"

Checking his pulse, I released a breath. "No, but we need to find supplies fast."

"We have to put some distance between us and here. How long can he last?" Adira bit her lip, looking at the cliffside.

"At best? Till morning," I replied honestly. "We need to get these wet clothes off him and move him somewhere where I can bandage him up."

Adira yelled to Eitan. Without questioning, he picked Raph up and carried him through a door near the front of the ship. The three of us followed.

Down the stairs were what looked to be personal living quarters. Eitan gently placed Raph on the bed carved into the side of the wall before taking off his wet clothes and putting a blanket over him.

When he was finished, I stepped toward the bed and set to work cleaning and wrapping his wound. He regained consciousness as I poured alcohol on it but passed out again shortly after. I was doing all I could with what I had, but my insides were knotted up, hating that I was not able to fully stitch him. When I finished, I stood staring at his serene face. A hand came to rest on my shoulder.

"You did good," Jules said from behind me. "Your mother would be proud."

Not taking my eyes off Raph, I wrapped my arms around my waist.

The door swung open. "I need to set a course," Gil stated, moving his gaze around the room, landing on Adira. She looked to Raph and then me.

"We need to find the nearest village," I said, scrunching my eyebrows together.

"Adira," Eitan said as almost a warning.

"I know," she snapped back.

"What is going on?" I asked.

"Set course to Aydencia," she commanded.

"Aydencia?" That wasn't a village in Landore. I turned to Jules expecting her to have the same look of confusion, but she stood with her head down. "Someone needs to tell me what's going on."

"Our mission was to get you to safety, Your Highness. The safest place for you is in Aydencia with our people—excuse me, *your* people," Eitan said calmly.

"My people? I don't have people. Where is this place?"

"The Northern Mountains," Adira stated.

My eyes widened. "You're the Northern Rebels?"

"That's a nickname the villagers gave us," Gil said with a flick of his hand.

My mind raced through everything I had learned about the rebels and also what I knew about the people in front of me. "But how? In the forest..."

"Can you believe that was a complete coincidence? We happened across the lost princess and didn't even know it!" Gil chuckled, leaning back against the door. He muttered something under his breath, but I couldn't hear it.

"We need to move. Madden will be on us soon," Eitan said to Adira, but his eyes flicked to Raph.

"Aydencia it is then." Gil pushed off the door.

"Wait!"

They all looked at me.

"I don't care what promise he made you guys make. We aren't going anywhere until he is stitched up."

"Is that a command, Your Highness?" Gil teased, but there was a sense of pride behind his eyes.

"Yes."

"I'll point us south." He gave a bow and a playful smirk before he slid out the door.

I expected Adira to be upset, but she had the same look Gil had. She made her way over to me and placed a hand on my shoulder. "You need to get out of those wet clothes, or you will be the next one who needs tending. Come with me. Eitan will look after him."

I peered down at Raph. Yes, our priority needed to be finding supplies. But after that, I needed to come up with another plan because I was not going to Aydencia.

THE END

THE CHOOSING

BOOK THREE IN THE CALLING SERIES

L.C. PYE

CHAPTER 1

Talia

"Raph. Wake up. Raph," I whispered.

His eyes blinked open as I touched his bare shoulder, giving it a slight shake.

"I need to stitch up your wound," I said, standing over him with a tight smile.

"It's fine," he said, pushing himself up, only to have a groan escape his lips.

"What do you think you're doing?"

His eyes, still heavy with sleep, looked at me through a few pieces of his hair. His gaze moved to the oversized green tunic Adira had given me. The muscles in his jaw tightened. "Seeing what the damage is," he said, propping himself up, and the blanket fell from his chest.

Heat traveled up my neck as I averted my eyes to the bandage I had wrapped around his waist. It was already bleeding through. He reached up to unwrap it.

"Stop," I said, taking a step closer. "Let me do it."

He paused. His hand contrasted against the dark bluish-purple color of the skin on top of his ribs.

"I think you might have a few broken ribs as well." I turned to grab the makeshift tray I had found with the supplies on it.

"Nothing I haven't dealt with before," he said with a raise of his shoulders.

"Does this happen a lot with what you guys do?" I asked, placing the tray on the edge of the bed.

"Let's just say this is not my first time being stitched up," he said while combing his fingers through his hair.

I shook my head and unwrapped the bandage.

He gave a sharp inhale as I peeled away the bloodied fabric.

"I'll be quick," I said as he laid back down.

He stayed focused on the ceiling as I got to work. He didn't give any signs of pain as I pushed the needle through his skin, but the tight grip he had on the blanket told me he wasn't immune to it.

"There," I said as I tied up the last stitch.

"You're really good at that." He peered down at the stitches. "It's a lot cleaner than the last stitch job I got."

I raised my brow, but he didn't indulge my curiosity. "I should be. I learned from the best Healer in Gasmere," I replied, placing the needle on the tray.

"What is she like, your mother?"

My back straightened. Turning away, I placed the tray and supplies onto the desk, trying to figure out the right words to say without ending up in tears. I took a seat at the end of the bed. "Mother is the most caring, selfless, and stern woman I have ever met. Both of my parents are wonderful," I added, unable to stop my lips from turning up. "They're kind and generous to everyone they meet. And I miss them dearly." My smile faltered as I looked down at my lap, not knowing if they were safe.

"You'll see them again."

"I have to. I can't live without them."

"You won't have to," he said, placing his hand on top of mine.

"What about your parents?" I asked cautiously.

"There really isn't that much to say. I never knew my father, and my mother loved me the best way she knew how. But she was always sick, and when I was seven, she passed away." He pulled his hand away, but I grabbed it and squeezed it between my own. His eyes lifted, guarded, ready to set up his walls. A small crease formed between my brows as I tried to look deeper, to piece together the countless puzzle pieces I had collected about him so far.

The door slammed against the wall, causing Raph and me to jump. Raph released a groan as I stood up.

"He lives! Trying to steal my job as the dramatic one?" Gil entered the room, perching himself against the desk.

"Wouldn't dream of it," Raph replied between his teeth as he pushed himself up to a sitting position.

"At least have the decency to put a shirt on." Gil propped one foot on the desk, then rested his elbow on his knee.

"Mind finding me one that isn't already being worn?" His eyes flicked to me briefly before returning back to Gil.

I pulled at the hem of my tunic, feeling heat flare to my cheeks.

"Glad to see you're back to normal," Adira said, throwing a shirt at Raph's face as she entered the room, followed by Jules and Eitan.

I moved closer to the door, near Jules.

"When will we reach Aydencia?" Raph asked while he pulled the shirt over his head stiffly. The room remained quiet. Raph zeroed in on Gil first before ending on Adira. "Well?"

"I ordered them to head to the nearest village to pick up supplies," I said with confidence, but my voice still seemed to get swallowed up by their stares. Jules gave me an encouraging nod. Taking a deep breath, I stepped forward. "And we have decided that before you take us to your hideout, we will be stopping in Gasmere."

"Is that so, Princess?" Raph's brow rose as he swung his feet to the floor.

"Yes," I said, bringing my hands to my hips. "King Madden is probably already on his way there. The village is in danger." I peered over my shoulder at Jules who was standing like a fierce warrior, but the slight bite of her lip gave her true feelings away. "He threatened to burn it to the ground if I disobeyed him." I looked back to Raph, "We have to warn them."

He didn't drop his stare until he released his breath, running his hand through his hair.

"We're less than a day from Gasmere," Gil stated.

Raph shook his head, then lifted his gaze. "We need to ensure her safety. The first place they will look is Gasmere. We head for Aydencia."

Jules stepped forward in line with me. "We can't let a whole village be burned to the ground."

"And we can't risk Madden getting his hands on the lost princess again," Raph replied.

"I'm right here," I said, waving my hands. "What if I say no to going to Aydencia? Will you threaten me like the king to get what you want?" My words came out harsher than I planned.

Raph's facade faltered as if my words had truly wounded him, "Tali—Princess, we are trying to protect you."

"If you really wanted to protect me, then you'd take me to Gasmere. Because that is my home. I don't just need physical protection. I need to know that they are safe."

"I thought you said someone had already extracted your parents?" Eitan asked. He was standing the closest to Jules and me with his arms crossed over his chest.

I'd given them all a brief rundown the night before of my experience with the Northern Rebels in the palace. "I never heard back that they were successful. That was almost a month ago."

"If Gale led it, I'm sure they got to them," Eitan stated.

"They are probably in Aydencia right now, waiting for you." Gil chimed in with a wide grin.

"I have to make sure." My throat swelled with unspoken fear.

The muscles in Raph's neck became visible. "Okay. We will head to Gasmere. But only Jules, Eitan, and Gil will go into the village. The three of us will wait at the closest safe house."

"Safe house?" Jules's voice hitched.

"Yes, we have multiple around Landore."

"We had this old girl stashed by the one nearest Lly-cia," Gil said, giving the side of the knarve a loving tap.

"Then after confirmation is made that your parents aren't there, and we warn the villagers, we will head to Aydencia." Raph pushed himself to standing by clutching onto the bedpost for support. "Do we have a deal, Princess?"

I smashed my lips into a straight line. "Yes."

"I will set a new course." Gil jumped from the desk already heading to the door. Eitan left next with Adira following right behind him.

I dashed out the door ahead of Jules, letting her close the door behind us. I didn't slow until my feet hit the top deck.

"Jules, want to help me secure the sail?" Adira yelled from further ahead.

"Are you good?" Jules asked as she reached out to me.

"I'm fine. Go," I replied, nodding my head to Adira.

Jules jogged over to where Eitan and Adira were already working on letting down the sail. A hole in my heart ached as I watched.

"We'll reach our destination before sundown," Gil informed me as I passed by the helm where he stood peering out into the distance with a spyglass. "Want a look?"

I placed the metal ring up to my eye. "I don't see anything," I said.

"Don't worry, you will soon."

I leaned my elbows against the railing and returned the spyglass. Raph made his way out from the stairwell, heading toward the other three. I looked away, knowing it would be pointless for me to try and order him back to bed. Instead, I focused on the white foam that came from the waves. It was a strange feeling, not being able to see anything but water around you. At times, if I stared for too long, my eyes would play tricks on me.

"Oy, land ahead," Gil shouted, cupping his hands to his mouth.

I rubbed my eyes then peered out again. The floating thing in the distance slowly morphed into a piece of land. Adira and Raph made their way up to the helm to join us.

"Keep us out for as long as you can," Raph said. He held out his hand to Gil who gave him the spyglass. "We can't afford to be spotted, especially since he knows we are traveling by water." Raph looked through it for a few moments before passing it to Adira.

"Ay-ay, Captain," Gil said with a mock salute. Raph raised his eyebrow, which made Gil break out with a satisfied grin. Adira offered me the spyglass. Greedily, I snatched it.

As my eyes focused, the small sliver of land I could see before was now magnified. It was a flat beach that raised ever so slightly the further back I looked. As I moved my focus further down the piece of land, I noticed something dark rising from it. It looked like a black cloud, but there were no other clouds in the sky.

"What's that?" I asked, pointing toward it.

"That area should actually be close to where Gasmere is located," Gil answered while throwing an arm around my shoulder.

"But what is that dark cloud over it? Is a storm coming?" I handed the spyglass to Gil.

He didn't say anything as he looked in the direction I had pointed and his arm dropped from my shoulder.

"Well?" I asked.

"Raph, take a look." Gil's voice dropped as he passed over the spyglass.

"What is it?" I looked at Gil who was still staring out in the same direction. With the naked eye, it appeared normal, only a tad bit darker than the rest of the blue sky.

"Smoke," Adira muttered.

"Yes," Raph confirmed.

"It can't be," I said, shaking my head. That would mean…" My stomach dropped. "No. No…" I grabbed Adira's hand. "Tell me it's not…" I pleaded.

"I…I'm sorry." Adira's eyes were full of regret.

A sob broke out. I covered my mouth as I fell to my knees. Eitan and Jules ran up the stairs, joining us.

"What's wrong?" Jules asked, making her way to me. Adira handed her the spyglass. "No!"

I stood back up. "We have to go. We have to help them." I said with unwavering determination.

"That's exactly where Madden is right now. He's probably doing this to lure you in." Raph turned away, descending the stairs, dismissing me.

"Raph, I'm not asking." I clenched my fists, letting the anger inside me rage on.

Raph's fists tightened as he turned to me.

"We don't know for sure if Madden will still be there," Gil offered, but Raph didn't release me from his stare.

"You will not leave my side." Raph spoke each word as a threat. "Understood?"

"Yes."

"Steer us to Gasmere, Gil." Raph broke his stare, storming down the stairs from the helm. I watched as he headed to the captain's cabin.

Adira's warm touch found my shoulder and gave me a squeeze. "He'll be fine. He puts too much pressure on himself. If anything were to happen to you, he would hold himself responsible."

"I understand. But he has to realize that I'll feel the same if anything happens to those I love." I pulled away from Adira and walked down the stairs to the front of the knarve.

It was getting easier to tell that the dark mass in the sky wasn't a cloud, but smoke. I had no idea what we would find. I tried to tell myself that maybe some trees caught on fire, or Gil got his coordinates wrong, but the sick feeling gnawing at my insides told me I needed to prepare for the worst.

We hadn't reached land till daybreak. Waiting all night had been excruciating. There was so much smoke. A thick layer of it covered the forest, resembling fog. We had our cloaks placed over our noses, trying not to breathe it in.

We walked for four hours, but I was thankful to do something physical. Plus, we were getting closer. The thickness of the smoke was the indicator of that.

"Hey," I called out from under my cloak. "Gasmere is a little southwest of here."

Raph, who was walking closer than necessary to me, gave me a nod of understanding. He turned to Eitan and tilted his head upward. The plan was for Eitan and Jules to enter from the Hunter's quarter, so Jules could check on her family. Raph was adamant that we get in and out as quickly as possible.

As the two of them veered off to the north, Adira and Gil flanked Raph and me on both sides.

"Make sure you bring us around the back, where we will be least visible," Raph muttered under his cloak. I nodded to confirm. I planned to bring us to the Farmer's quarter where the fields were.

As we crept closer to the boundaries of Gasmere, my chest tightened, and I couldn't shake the urge to run. A part of me still hoped it was an accidental fire or maybe a forest fire like the one that had happened when I was a girl. The whole village had to help to prevent it from spreading into the town or the fields. It had taken days before the smoke disappeared.

I gasped and dropped the cloak from my mouth.

It was all gone.

Past the fields, I could only see the remains of where there were once multiple Farmers' homes. Some were completely gone with only black ash left as evidence of their existence while others had some of their frame-work still standing.

I sprinted toward my home, praying that something would be left, that my parents would be there un-harmed. I heard my name being called, but I was fo-cused on one thing. Running down the familiar road, I couldn't stop tears from streaming as I took in the state of the homes. The quarter was destroyed. There was nothing left.

In my heart, I knew what I should expect to see, but a part of me couldn't help but hope. I had to see it for myself. Throat burning, I pushed down the sobs and walked into the remains of my childhood home.

Smoke rose from a few areas, so it couldn't have been more than a day since this happened. I stepped into the kitchen where the only things still recognizable were a few metal pots and the onyx stove. Everything else was ash or unrecognizable. I picked up a bowl and clutched it to my chest as I fell to my knees. What had I done?

"Talia," someone called, followed by the sound of footsteps.

I clutched the bowl tighter as I stared at the ash around me. Adira kneeled and placed her arm around me.

This was my fault. Another sob racked through me.

"Welcome home, Princess."

I jumped, dropping the bowl with a thud, to clench my fists as I turned around to face that all too familiar voice.

BONUS CHAPTER OF PRINCE KASPER'S POV

Want to know what Prince Kasper was thinking when King Madden announced his engagement to Talia?

Receive the bonus chapter by signing up to my mailing list.

Get it here!

ACKNOWLEDGMENTS

The Finding would never have been written without the help of so many people, many of whom are unaware of their influence.

All honor and credit goes to my Heavenly Father. He gave me the strength to carry on when I felt unworthy and ill-equipped to write a book. This book is only possible because of Him.

I have to thank my husband, Matt, who has supported me through every up and down, helping me pursue this dream by being my biggest supporter. Love you so much, babe, always and forever. My family has always been and will continue to be my biggest supporters (even though they really have no choice). I am extremely grateful for every one of them.

To my readers: I don't know how to show you my gratitude. Your support and love of *The Calling* has helped motivate me to continue on. It's not easy being an author and having your work constantly judged but knowing that my book resonated with readers means the world to me. Your excitement for this series is infectious. Thank you for believing in me. I hope you have enjoyed *The Finding* even more than book one! If you have, please SHARE the love with others. The best way to support me is to spread the word to your friends or with a review on Amazon or Goodreads. Also, please reach out. I would love to know your thoughts and get to know you!

My mystery beta reader, where do I even start? Jade Lawson, I could talk you up for hours. You're a true blessing, and I'm forever grateful you reached out about being a beta reader for book one. I can't wait to see where this series goes with your help. Thank you for your honest feedback and advice.

My editor, Brittany Ortega at E&A Editing Services, was incredible and brought this book to a whole new level. I was so excited to work with her again, and she did not disappoint. She tightened up my writing and assisted this book in becoming the best it could be. Thank you for your constant support and belief in my writing!

About Author
L.C. Pye

L.C. Pye is a South Carolina-based author of YA novels. She grew up in North Dakota, then moved to Australia for four years after college. She met her husband there, and in 2018, they moved to the Carolinas. She has spent most of her life creating stories through the art of dance. But after a dream in 2019, she decided to try telling her stories through words.

L.C. has had the privilege of traveling to many different countries, and she loves to put those differing but beautiful cultures into her writing. She hopes all her readers will experience the same beauty she has.

Connect with L.C.
Website: www.lcpye.com
Instagram: @l.c.pye
TikTok: @l.c.pye
Email: authorl.c.pye@gmail.com

www.ingramcontent.com/pod-product-compliance
Lightning Source LLC
Chambersburg PA
CBHW021224310726
48971CB00006B/1676